A KEY, A GARDEN, A COTTAGE

A mystery lies within

By Jean Kirby

New Generation Publishing

Also by Jean Kirby

Cancer The Heartache The Truth
Three Ways to Die

THE HIDDEN SECRET

**She thought she knew him, but his secret past catches up with him.
She goes on a road of discovery**

GREEN WITH ENVY

**Her jealousy eats away at her when she and her husband go to work on the Estate.
She realises she wants more, like the owners, but how low will she stoop?**

THE MAGIC TOUCH

She only wanted a pretty cottage to settle into but did not expect what she found.

THE HIDDEN SECRET

Chapter 1

The phone rang. It was the police to say her husband had been in a car crash and he had been rushed to hospital, but as his face was so damaged they could not identify him from his ID that was in the car with him. They needed her to come to the hospital to make the identification.

Adrenaline shot through her body. She was trying to think as quickly as she could. Yes, she could meet the police at the hospital and identify her husband to confirm it was him, but how? Of course; his ring, his tattoo. She was scared and unsure what she would find.

She grabbed her coat, handbag and car keys and left the house. Her heart was beating so fast she could hardly breathe. She needed to calm down, slow her breathing. What had he done this time?

She knew he had a mysterious past when she fell in love with him. He was very cagey about what he did for a job, but said now he had steady employment as an Accountant and had a house, when he met her. He said he wanted to settle down.

They had a whirlwind romance and within six months they married and the honeymoon period certainly continued once they were married. She understood not to discuss his past as he had told her it was very painful for him so she respected his request. It never affected their relationship in any way. They lived in a farmhouse in a village close to a larger town of Haythorpe. This was where he had gone to in the car so she was surprised when the police told her where the car had crashed, going in the total opposite direction.

Could the police be mistaken with the car registration, was it his car? She was confused. She arrived at the hospital, parked and went into A&E and asked for the police, who were waiting for her.

She hesitated when they directed her to a screened area where he was. They had cleaned his body up as best they could and she was warned to expect the worst by the hospital doctor. She turned to the police officer who was also with her and asked, "Was he wearing a seat belt?"

The officer replied, "No the seat belt was not fastened and the air bag failed to go off as well, that's why his face is so damaged."

She sighed. That was not like him. Was he distracted or had he stopped somewhere and then when he got back in forgot to do his belt up? No that could not be him, anyway modern cars alert you about not fastening your seat belt. Then the issue of the air bag not activating at all sounded alarming. It was not adding up.

She was ready, she thought, so nodded to them both and was taken into the cubicle to see him. She squeezed her eyes so that she would not see properly and frighten herself straight away. She moved nearer to the top of the bed. Slowly she relaxed her eyes to allow herself to see what was in front of her. A shiver went up her spine. She sensed his body was different as she cast her eyes over the covered figure in front of her. Could it be someone like Alex, she needed to check the ring and tattoo. She asked to see the top of his left arm. But wait that was the same tattoo and then his hand had the ring she had placed there herself when they got married which he never removed. She was stunned. She felt faint and the doctor caught her and got her to a chair just in time.

4

She felt her chest tighten, her hands clammy. She tried to take a deep breath while the doctor by her side tried to tell her what to do. She couldn't hear him, the words didn't register. She was in a fog, her feet in quick sand, she felt as if she was drowning, then blackness.

When she opened her eyes she was on a bed in a cubicle with a nurse checking her vital signs. The nurse spoke to her, "You passed out for five minutes, we were worried about you but everything seems to have settled back to normal now but please lie still as you have had a tremendous shock." Lucy swallowed and then thanked her. She looked around and tried to think through what had happened in the time she came to the hospital. Yes now she remembered, the body she saw was it actually her husband?

Lucy would have to confirm with the police that it was him even if she was not 100% sure but everything was pointing to the fact it was him. She had to go through with it in case Alex was in trouble of some sort. She said she was okay now to talk to the police and shortly after an officer came in to see her. He introduced himself and started asking questions. He asked, "The body you were shown can you confirm that it was your husband Alex George Hutchins."

Lucy answered, "Yes, it is." He went on to say there were a few other things that needed to be done and then his body would be released to her. Did she have a funeral director they could contact on her behalf and they could get them to collect the body for her. He also said they would be testing the car for faults. She thanked the officer who then left.

Her mind was racing now. She had to organise a funeral, but why doubts in her mind? It was him.

When she first met him he would not say what his job was as he was not allowed to talk about it, even to his wife. She thought maybe he was working for MI5 or the SAS but he would not tell her anything about his work before he met her. She would go ahead with the funeral and hope everything would work out, but just in case he had been working for MI5 still, she would be on her guard. She hated not knowing what the truth was. Was he safe somewhere or had he been murdered? She had to put on a brave face for everyone.

The doctor came in with the nurse and said that she was now okay to go now and asked about her husband's body. She said she knew the funeral director she would use, it was someone she used when her mum died. She said she would ring the hospital when she got home with the details. The doctor gave her details on which person to ring to collect the body.

She collected his things and left the hospital, putting her sun glasses on as it seemed bright outside. She looked around at people as she walked to her car but no one looked suspicious or what she assumed did. This was new to her and she had no idea what or who she was looking for.

She got in the car and locked the doors. Was she getting paranoid? She had to act naturally. She drove home checking her mirror more than normal, drove up the drive and parked, turned the engine off and let her head rest on the steering wheel. A tap on the window made her jump. She looked up and saw her neighbour looking through the window concerned.

Lucy got out of the car as June her neighbour asked, "Are you okay? I was worried about you, you left so early."

Lucy replied, "Yes my husband has been killed in a car accident." June looked surprised and passed on her condolences, then asked if she could help her in any way. Lucy asked her to come into the house and she would explain what had happened. They went into the house and straight to the kitchen to put the kettle on. June followed her in.

"He is dead?" June asked. "I can't believe it."

"Can I help you in any way? Just ask."

Lucy thought for a second and said it would be good to have someone holding her hand through this journey of the unknown. June took over the making of tea while Lucy found the number of the funeral directors and rang them explaining what was required. They wanted to come and see her to go over the details of the funeral etc. and she suggested in a couple of days-time to allow her to get her head around things. A date and time was agreed and looking at June she nodded and mouthed that was okay with her.

She put the telephone down and June handed her a mug of tea. She sat down and had a sip of tea. She was hungry now and said to June she would make them both a sandwich. When she brought the sandwiches in for them to eat she told June about what had happened at the hospital and how she now needed to organise the funeral. She made a list of people to contact while eating her sandwich and drinking her tea. She felt better now, more focused.

Lucy opened a bottle of wine. She needed a drink now and decided on her plan of action which she would start tomorrow. They had many friends scattered across the country and Alex was short on family so only a couple to contact. June said she would help out with the telephoning of people and arranged a time for her to come over tomorrow.

June started gently asking for more details on the accident trying not to pry too much but she needed to be sure that it was Lucy's husband. Her bosses would be wanting a report from her as they had been monitoring Alex for some time, in fact since he got married. Lucy gave her as much information as the police had given her and as she said to June, "He had my ring I put on his finger when we married and his tattoo, so it was him for sure." Lucy thought a little, and came to the conclusion that even though she was friendly with June she seemed to be asking a lot of questions. Anyway she felt exhausted and asked June to leave and she was sure she would see her tomorrow.

After she had gone she went into Alex's study and started looking around. She did not know what she was looking for but she knew something was wrong. She found files of accounts, papers, familiar and some not so familiar names, locked draws of the desk. She attempted to look for a key to open it but having not being successful took the letter opener to force it open. Inside she came across a set of keys. She looked around to see what she could open with them but drew a blank. She would sleep on it and maybe in the morning she would look around for something the keys would open.

She locked up and went upstairs and upon opening the door to the bedroom, saw the empty bed. That's when reality hit her and hard. She fell onto the bed crying. Thinking to her-self where was he? Could she find him? Did he want to be found? Or was that really him? So many unanswered question and she was so emotional she did not know what to believe. She managed to get herself into bed and cuddling the pillow. She fell asleep.

The next morning she woke with a splitting headache, her mouth felt dry. Dehydration, she thought to herself, she needed to drink lots of water and take some tablets. She dragged herself into the shower, letting the warm water breathe life into her. Once dressed she went down to the kitchen, drank two glasses of water, after which she felt better and started organising some breakfast for herself.

After she had eaten she took a mug of coffee along with a glass of water into the lounge to start making a list of who to contact for the funeral. It seemed weird that she was planning his funeral when she was not sure it was him, but she needed to believe it was him, she was being silly. The Funeral Director was due to ring her with a date so she would hold off ringing people until then, but still needed to make a list. Things progressed and the list grew as she found herself drinking her third mug of coffee when the doorbell rang. She sat upright for a second with heart racing, wondering who could it be, and then realised it would be her neighbour June.

Lucy opened the door. Yes it was her, as she stood in front of her all smiles. She enquired how Lucy had slept and had anybody rung her yet. Lucy replied that no one as yet had been in touch and June looked disappointed. Lucy wondered why. Strange lady she thought. Lucy told her to get a coffee from the kitchen and then she could help with collecting the telephone numbers of people she needed to contact. This took all morning until they had everybody that needed to know, and the people who would want to attend the funeral.

They stopped to have some lunch, just a sandwich, and over it they exchanged small talk to take Lucy's mind off things. They were just having a coffee afterwards when the telephone rang and Lucy went to pick it up. It was the Funeral Directors. They had picked up the body from the hospital that morning and he was now in their care. He would be round tomorrow morning to organise the arrangements with her but she needed a date. She pushed him and he said he could do it in ten days' time but would confirm the details with her tomorrow. She put the telephone down and decided she would ring the ones she knew would not come to the funeral first, and the others she would ring tomorrow once she knew where and when it would take place.

They shared the calls and would not leave any messages, and marked at the side of the paper whether they needed to ring again. This was thirsty work and June got up to make some tea for them when Lucy glanced down at the list and a name jumped out at her, her husband's boss. Why had he not rung her? Strange, she thought, he would have known her husband was due in for work? She needed to speak to him to find out what he knew. She dialled his number. It rang three times and was answered by a female saying the name of the Company and could she help. Lucy asked to speak to Mr Hardman who was Alex's boss, but she was not sure what his first name was. The secretary said she would put her through.

A soft spoken man answered and said, "Hello Lucy I was surprised to hear from you as Alex said he was taking you away for a few days' holiday to Paris."

She was shocked at what he had said but recovered to answer, "Yes we were, but before we were due to set off, Alex had to run an errand in the car and ended up crashing it, but I am sorry to say it was a fatal accident and he died."

She heard a sharp intake of breathe on the line, then he cleared his throat and replied, "I am so sorry to hear that, please accept my condolences and if I can help in any way please do not hesitate to ask."

She felt like shouting down the telephone, where the hell is my husband but she calmed herself and replied, "That is very kind of you, but would you or anyone in the office want to come to the funeral? I will give you the time and place once I have it confirmed."

He said he would ring her with the number of people and also get the details from her then. She put the telephone down and put her head in her hands. June walked in with a tray of tea and then Lucy looked up and thought should she share what she had found out, no, to be on the safe side she would keep it to herself. June asked who it was and Lucy fobbed her off by saying just another name off the list. They had the tea and then June apologised and said she needed to go. Lucy thanked her for all her help and said it was okay not to come round when the Funeral Director came as she could cope. June asked, was she sure and Lucy reiterated she was fine. She had dealt with her mother's death last year and knew what she was doing.

Lucy shut the door behind June as she left and felt she must push on with the telephoning, another hour should be enough. It did take a little longer but all were eventually done. She sighed and felt a little better now.

She decided she needed a glass of wine with her dinner as she felt she deserved it for all the hard work she had done. After eating she sat down in the lounge with her second glass of wine and looked at her car keys on the coffee table. It reminded her of the keys she had found that belonged to Alex. What or where would they lead her to she thought. Maybe she would start at the Bank. They had safety deposit boxes no doubt even in this modern age. She went and collected the keys from the study where she had put them and brought them back. She put them on the table and thought to herself are they the right looking keys for a safety deposit box? She was unsure.

Distracted, her mind wandered. She must ring the Solicitor up about the will and sort the financial situation out now that Alex was dead. She looked at the keys on the table again, picking them up and turning them in her fingers wanting them to reveal their secret to her there and then. She put them down and took a sip of wine. She should put them away safely maybe in her bedroom. She stood up, picked them up and started towards the hall when the door-bell rang. She quickly put them in her pocket and went to the door.

Lucy opened the door and there stood a tall, dark haired and rather handsome stranger.

"Can I help you?" she said. He cleared his voice and said, "I am sorry to bother you but after our conversation this afternoon I felt I needed to call and pay my respects. I am Dean Hardman, Alex's boss." He put his hand out and she shook it and then gestured for him to come in.

Lucy felt very wary but also comfortable at the same time. She led him into the lounge and offered him a drink, which he declined. They sat opposite each other. Dean started talking about Alex and his job with the Company and said he was a hard worker and was due to be made partner shortly. He also mentioned that they'd known each other at school before they went their separate ways, Dean to University and Alex to work at the family business. Lucy was intrigued as Alex had never really talked about his childhood so she asked Dean more about their childhood together. He continued to talk quite openly about when they were boys at school and what they got up to.

She offered Dean a coffee again and this time he said yes and followed her into the kitchen while she made it and he continued talking about their childhood together. Lucy asked what the family business was and Dean said a garage, as Alex loved cars and engines especially when he took them to bits and was able to put them all back again correctly. Dean said he would always call at the family garage if he had problems with his car. Dean went on to say that was when they lost touch with each other, as Alex's family took the business out of town and away from the area. It was only by chance they met in a bar six years ago.

Alex had qualified as an accountant late in his career, and had not found a firm to take him on. Dean was looking to expand his firm and that is how he came to work for him. Lucy told Dean that Alex had not told her a lot, only that he was working for this firm, Dean's, not the history behind the job. They had only been married three years but thought Alex would have told her that who he was working for was an old school friend. Lucy was feeling comfortable in Dean's company and decided to ask a strange question. "Dean, did you think Alex was hiding anything, however strange it may have been?"

Dean thought for a while, "I am not sure but he would go away for days not weeks, he would change the colour of his hair a lot and would have beards, hair growth on his chin, always changing his appearance. He would just laugh it off and say he was going through a mid- life crisis! It stopped when he met you strangely enough."

Lucy said, "That's interesting and did he go away on behalf of the Company to conferences in the last three years as well?"

Dean looked puzzled, "No we had a department head that went to most of them as Alex was more client based", Dean replied, feeling he was missing something, but felt it was not his place to pry into their private life just yet.

Dean felt he had stayed too long and said he must be going. He told Lucy he would be at the funeral and if she needed anything to get in touch with him. She thanked him and closed the door as he left. She sighed as she leant against the door. What should she do now? She needed to get the funeral out of the way first and then start digging for clues as to what had happened to Alex and what he was actually doing.

Chapter 2

The morning of the funeral could not have been more depressing. It was cold, raining and windy. Alex had no living relatives, just friends, she had a sister who was not close but was there to support her and lots of close friends she had accumulated over the years. The service was as she arranged and she shed a tear. She did not know why, but this poor fellow she was burying was not her husband, that was for sure she thought. He had to be buried whether he was her husband or not.

Most of the congregation attended the graveside and Dean came up to her, took both her hands, which he held for a few seconds before he said how sorry he was. She smiled at him and thanked him, but her eyes were drawn to look over his shoulder to notice a stranger standing away from the grave. He had a hat, dark glasses and a long dark coat. Who was he? Dean noticed where her eyes went and looked over to where the man stood, who upon being aware he had been spotted started to walk towards a car. Dean turned back to Lucy and mouthed to her leave it to him.

The rain had stopped as they made their way from the cemetery to the hotel for the wake. She greeted people as they arrived and thanked them for coming, and when everyone had arrived she walked over and picked up a drink and made her way to the buffet. She was hungry. She spoke to people as she walked around and then noticed Dean appear at the doorway so went over to him and greeted him when he said, "We need to talk in private, soon please."

"Okay that's not a problem," she said, not

knowing what he meant, and he went off to talk to his colleagues who had come with him. After a while people started leaving with Lucy again thanking people who had come. Soon she was alone and was just looking to phone for a taxi when she turned round and Dean was standing there. He had come back for her to take her home and would not take no for an answer.

She followed him to the car and he opened the door for her to get in, closing it behind her then getting in. He drove to her house in silence, drove up the driveway and turned the engine off and got out to come round to her side to open the door for her. As he opened the door he said, "We need to talk, would now be a good time or would you prefer me to come back later in the week?"

She thought for a second and said, "No, now is as good a time than any." She needed to know what he knew and she could not wait any longer.

Dean locked the car and followed her into the house. She went straight to the kitchen and took a bottle of red wine, opened it, poured two glasses and handed him one of them. Lucy took a sip and felt better then said, "Who was that man at the cemetery?"

Dean frowned. What should he tell her and would it make her more afraid? No he had to tell her and see how she handles it. He took a sip of wine and started to tell her. He said after he left the graveside he followed the guy heading for the car, which they had both seen. He took the registration down and then went to his car to follow. He lost the car at a set of traffic lights heading out of town. He went on to say he had contacted a friend that worked with the police to see if they could trace the registration number for him. He said the friend could not promise but would come back to him if he could find out anything. Dean asked Lucy had she seen the man before and she replied, "Not as far as I could tell." He thought it was very strange and said that could it have been someone who bore a grudge against Alex at work or socially but Lucy pointed out that she had only known Alex for a few years and said he did not want to talk about his past. This, she thought, was because he had painful memories.

They both went into the lounge and sat down sipping their drink when they both said together, "What was he hiding?" They both laughed.

Lucy said, "Can I confide in you and tell you, I don't think I buried Alex today!" Dean was not sure how to react. She identified the body so how could that be.

He said to Lucy, "Why would you say that after what you have done today, buried your husband?"

She went on to explain about Alex saying he was going into the village for something but the car was found in the opposite direction a long distance away. He had no seat belt on and the air bag did not work, it was as if someone had wanted to destroy evidence of his identity. Yes the body had his tattoo and wedding ring but nothing else she recognised. Dean said, "That must have been terrible for you." She nodded. Then she went on with her story. He never mentioned about a trip to Paris and only that he had a few days off and wanted to do some jobs around the house. They both looked puzzled. What was Alex hiding neither of them was sure. Lucy decided to confide in Dean about the keys.

She said, "After I came home from the hospital I went into Alex's study and searched for any clues that might help me. I discovered a locked draw in the desk and decided to force it open and discovered three sets of keys."

Dean looked thoughtful and then said, "Have you thought it might be for a safety deposit box at the bank."

Lucy said, "Yes that was one thing I was thinking of to start as I need to go to the bank to sort out the financial situation with his death." She went on to say they actually had separate bank accounts as she had been left a large amount of money by her parents which Alex did not want to touch.

Dean said he could come with her tomorrow afternoon to the bank if she wanted and she said that would be good to have the support of someone else there. They agreed a time and would meet outside the bank rather than him coming and collecting her at the house. She had nosey neighbours and did not want her neighbours asking questions. It was agreed then. Dean excused himself and decided he needed to leave at this point moving to the door which she opened he turned and taking her hands in his said, "We will work it out and find the truth one way or another about your husband." Then turned and left.

Lucy closed the door and decided it had been a long day and she needed a long soak in the bath and bed. Sleep was easy. As soon as her head hit the pillow she was asleep only to have her dreams become nightmares. She saw gun battles, weird creatures and yes her husband's face everywhere. She suddenly woke from one of these nightmares and found herself covered in sweat. She lay awake for a few minutes before she fell asleep again as she was so exhausted.

Sunlight streaming through the window woke her.

She looked at the clock, eight o'clock. She needed a shower to wake herself up and as she felt she had not slept well last night maybe a cold one! She needed to dress and had things to do before meeting Dean at the bank.

After she showered and dressed she went downstairs and had some breakfast in the kitchen. She felt hungry as she only nibbled at the food at the wake. She was just enjoying a slice of toast – with chocolate spread and bananas – when the knock on the door came. It was June from next door. She had been at the funeral but not at the wake. She opened the door, saw June but looked past her to see a removal van on her drive. She said hello and would she like to come in for a coffee but June declined saying she was moving as the landlord wanted the house back to move into the house himself. She said she knew about it a few weeks ago but did not want to mention it because of what happened.

Lucy thanked her for all her help over the last few weeks and asked where she was moving to, but June would not tell her, only that she might move back with her parents for the time being and that she would be in touch once she was settled. Lucy wished her luck and closed the door. Well, she thought, that was unexpected, a bolt out of the blue. Had she only moved in just to watch Alex and now he was dead she was moving on? Something she needed to tell Dean perhaps when they met up later.

After her breakfast she poured a coffee for herself and went into the study, sat on Alex's chair at his desk and studied the room. What was she looking for she did not know, only that this study held secrets he kept from her. As she cast her eyes around the room two books looked out of place, whether it was size or shape she was not sure. She stood up and went over to them when a shiver went down her spine, silly her. She touched the books but was surprised to find they were false ones and fixed together. She pulled at them and a secret drawer revealed itself and she jumped back in surprise. It was two shelves below where she was standing. She peered inside to find different types of weapons, from guns to knives and small books which when she flicked through the pages revealed code numbers and drawings and symbols. This did not make sense to her, and she was too scared to look any further, so she pushed the books again and the secret drawer closed. What was Alex involved in?

She sat back in his chair and drank her coffee, still glancing around the room. She thought nothing else looked unusual and then looked at the desk top and saw an ornament she had not noticed before, and could not remember it from anywhere they had been together. She held it in her hands. It reminded her of the Chinese puzzle boxes you could buy, in fact like the one her father used to bring home from his travels around the world. Turning it, and pushing and pulling it, she eventually opened it to reveal the desk drawer key, the one she had to force open.

Lunchtime had come around quickly as she was so pre-occupied in the Study. She made herself a small sandwich before going off to the bank to meet up with Dean. She made sure she took all the keys and wished that one would work to see what had been hidden away and give her some answers. She grabbed her coat and car keys and left the house for the bank.

When she arrived outside the bank Dean was not there. Maybe he had been delayed so she went into the bank to deal with the other paperwork that needed doing with Alex's death. Once that was done she asked to see the safety deposit box they had, and was asked to wait while she informed someone else who would deal with it. While she was waiting Dean turned up apologising for being late. She quickly told him that she would introduce him as her Solicitor when they took them down to where the safety deposit boxes were. Dean nodded in agreement.

A few minutes later someone took them to a downstairs room and showed them to a box on a table stating that it was hers and they would leave them to open it. Lucy took the keys out of her handbag and laid them on the table. She tried the first one, it did not fit, then the second one and yes that went in and turned to hear it click open the lock. Her heart was racing. Dean said, "Come on, open it we both want to know what's inside." She gingerly opened the lid to reveal not what she was expecting. She pulled out the first item which was a jewellery case which she opened to reveal a diamond pendant. She had forgotten about it. He had bought it for her on their first wedding anniversary and she had scolded him for buying something so expensive for her. He had insisted that she wear it but because of her concern about the insurance not covering it he said he would find a safe place for it. Maybe he told her and she forgot, she could not remember.

When Dean saw it he whistled and said, "Wow that is worth a lot of money."

Lucy replied, "I don't know how much but I think it is best I leave it here for safe keeping."

There was an envelope with her name on it at the bottom of the box which she took out and opened. She realised it was from Alex in case of his death instructing her where certain documents were in the Study. Then further down the letter were some symbols against single words. She showed that part to Dean which he thought might indicate some form of coded message to her but she would need the code to read it. They were both unsure what it meant.

Lucy put the letter in her handbag and looked at the empty box. She put the jewellery case back in and closed the lid, locked it and rang a bell for someone to collect them and take the box back into their care. They thanked the staff and before they left the bank Lucy asked for Dean to come round to the house about 8pm if he could so they can talk further over what they had found. Dean said that was fine and they both left.

Driving home she thought should she have asked him to stay for dinner but no that was too forward she thought to herself. When she got home she was hungry so started making dinner from scratch which she had not done for a long time. She enjoyed cooking and was very inventive in the kitchen. When she had finished cooking she sat down to eat it, feeling very pleased with herself as she sipped from her glass of red wine.

After eating she went into the lounge and took out the envelope she had picked up from the bank and went into the Study. She put it down on the desk and went over to where the secret drawer was and pulled the books to open it. There were four small books in the draw so she picked them up and brought them over to the desk where the letter was.

She had a large writing pad so she could write on anything that resembled clues to the codes in the letter. She tried to match up anything from the books to the symbols in the letter and wrote down the words. She was not sure what she was doing but it felt the right way to start with it. She must have been doing this for an hour or so when the door-bell rang, that would be Dean she thought. She got up, closed the door to the Study, and went to answer the door.

She opened the door and found Dean standing on the door step. She invited him in and he gave her a bottle. She thanked him and asked if he wanted a drink to which he said yes so they went into the kitchen to get a glass when he said, "Something smells nice, dinner was it?"

"Yes," replied Lucy, "I cooked it myself and I had forgotten how much I enjoyed doing it as well."

He took the glass from her and she topped up hers which she had brought out of the Study with her and they went to sit in the lounge. Lucy explained to Dean how she had been trying to work out the symbols in the letter that Alex left her and that she was not getting very far. Dean said she probably needed a code book to help connect the figures and symbols. That was when Lucy said, "Well actually I found something hidden in Alex's study which might help along with other items."

Dean looked quizzical, "What do you mean?"

She said, "I'll show you, bring your drink with you and we'll go in the study."

They headed for the study and she opened the door and walked to the desk with Dean following and pointed to the open drawer by the bookcase. Dean was speechless at what he saw, guns and knives. What was Alex up to? He went nearer for a closer look. He turned towards Lucy who was now at the desk, "How did you find this?"

Lucy said, "By accident when looking at the books and the two being out of place, touching them and the secret drawer opened."

He came over to the desk now and looked at the

strange books open at pages with symbols and writing in them. Lucy asked him to sit and she would show him what she had so far. They looked at the book and then the letter, trying to decipher what they meant. Dean loved puzzles and was identifying and matching things up. After about an hour between them they thought they had found a meaning behind each one but now they needed to make it make sense. Directions to somewhere, access to more information, or to where they can use the keys that were left?

They decided that they were in no order, therefore the meaning had to be something Alex and she knew from their time together. They went over and over all sorts of things but nothing rang any bells with Lucy. Dean suggested she sleep on it and maybe a fresh start in the morning might jog her memory. They put the books back in the secret drawer and closed it with Dean watching and then both went into the kitchen to top up the glasses. They talked and Dean said he thought he knew Alex but now he was unsure from what they had found and Lucy agreed. She needed answers to so many questions about him but needed to sleep on it.

They went to the lounge and sat down, making small talk, when Dean said he thought he should go after a while. She showed him to the door. He left her closing the door behind her and her wanting to go to bed now as she was tired and hopefully would feel refreshed in the morning.

Chapter 3

It was a couple of days late she telephoned Dean at the office. They exchanged greetings and asked how each other was. Then Lucy asked if he was free that evening to come over for some dinner and discuss what she thought might be the answer to the clues they had found, and for Dean to agree or shoot them down as silly. He said he had a late meeting but could be round at 7pm if that was okay with her. She said fine but had he any dislikes when it came to food and he said he was fairly easy going when it came to food. She said she would see him later.

She arrived home after shopping for food for that evening. She thought she would do antipasti to start with then a simple prawn and spinach pasta dish, and a desert which she bought in case they were still hungry. She put everything away till later and walked into the study and looked at what she had written down from the last two days. She had a few ideas about what they might mean but really was not sure, she needed Dean's help. She stopped for a moment. He was good looking and he was not pushing his attention on her in any way so she did not feel threatened by him. Anyway she did not know if her husband was still alive. She dismissed her thoughts of Dean at that point.

The evening came and she had changed into comfortable trousers and top, make-up and hair done. She had prepared everything she could and was just putting the last touches to the antipasti when the door-bell rang. She went and opened the door and Dean stood there with a bottle and a small box of chocolates. He said they were for desert and winked at her. He jokingly said that all the ladies he meets say they are on a diet so by taking chocolates at least he gets to eat them. She laughed.

She took him into the lounge where she had laid out what she thought she had found out about the symbols and numbers. Dean looked at them with interest. He asked, "Do you have a map at all of the country or local area that you may have used when you went out together somewhere?"

She said, "Yes we would always take a map as Alex hated the sat-nav. It is in the study, I will go and fetch it."

She brought back the map and he spread it out on the table and looked at the numbers then the map. Lucy was pointing to different places they used to go to and visit together when she saw it and jabbed her finger on the place. "That's it, we went there maybe six months ago, and had a lovely meal there." Dean looked at the numbers. Yes they converged on the village of Mayburn.

They looked at the symbols which now made sense to Lucy, a pub they went to in the village what was it, Crown or Kings Head or Queens Head or maybe the other symbols the Sun or the Keys. They needed to go to the village and see which one and maybe it would jog her memory. They put everything away in the study and came and sat down in the lounge together. He said how well she looked and asked what had she been up to. She asked him had he heard from his friend in the police about the car.

He said he had heard nothing but they did work slowly. They then went into the kitchen to eat where she had laid a cloth over a small bistro table she had in the kitchen, which was better than eating in the dining room as it was too formal.

He sat down as she brought out the anti-pasta over to the table, along with the bottle of wine. He said how lovely it looked and then went on to talk about his love of food and cooking. Dean went on to say that his cooking was hit and miss. It depended when he had time. The evening passed quickly but they both decided to go for the desert and ate it up with relish. They adjourned to the lounge afterward for coffee and Dean insisted they have a chocolate with it as well which they both laughed about.

After a while he said he needed to ring for a taxi home and she let him do so and after 10 minutes it arrived and they were saying their goodbyes when Dean gently kissed her on the cheek and thanked her for a lovely evening. They agreed as he left that she would follow up on the information about possibly being in a village she once visited and let him know what she found. She would ring him next evening to let him know.

She shut the door and locked up as she needed to go to bed. Climbing the stairs she felt tired but happy that maybe they were finding more out about Alex. She hoped she would sleep well tonight and look forward to tomorrow.

The next day she set off on her journey of discovery. She hoped it would jog her memory and bring back happy ones of her and Alex. She arrived at Mayburn and found a car park. She grabbed her coat and bag and headed for the high street. When she arrived she walked up and down hoping something would look familiar and jog her memory. After a while she decided just to go window shopping at all the lovely shops available on the high street.

The first one she stopped at and looked into the window. It was a jewellery shop. She looked at the display of diamond rings and that reminded her of the bracelet he wanted to buy her and she had told him it was too expensive for her to wear. But he insisted it would match the diamond necklace he had bought her. She told him it would be silly as she hardly wore that and it would be the same for the bracelet. She eventually talked him out of it.

She lifted her eyes up away from the window and glanced across the road. There it was, an old hanging sign of a pub, the Queens Head, but the building was now occupied by a bank but next door was a pub called the Sun. She remembered now they had lunch in there. She crossed the road and went into the bank and found an assistant. She asked if they had safety deposit boxes as she wanted to put some jewellery into one but thought her late husband had actually acquired one here. The assistant checked the records but said that she would require identification documents before she could give her any more information. She gave her a card so she could ring and make an appointment for her to come back and look at the deposit box. She thanked the assistant and left the bank.

Lucy came out of the bank and decided to go to The Sun for lunch for old time sake. She had a lovely ploughmans lunch and when she finished she headed to the car park. She got into the car and while heading home decided to ring Dean to see what his movements were, before she rang the bank to make an appointment. She dialled his number on her hands-free phone and got through to his direct line he had given her. She apologised for bothering him at work and said that if she knew his movements she could arrange an appointment with the bank. She filled in the details of why and what she had found on her trip.

He said he could only do late tomorrow and that she should go alone unless she wanted another time. She said she would get back to him.

When she got home she rang the bank to make arrangements for an appointment to see the safety deposit box tomorrow. It was possible to make it as late as possible just on the off chance Dean could make it. She was hoping one of the other keys would open it up and reveal its secrets and give her some answers. After she had finished the call she went into the kitchen to make herself a cup of coffee. She sat down in the lounge, deep in thought, when the phone rang and made her jump. It was the police to say that the results were back about the accident and the car. It was inconclusive what had happened and they were in talks with the manufacturer to see if any faults had occurred on other models, and agreed there was no foul play involved, but mechanical failure was the fault. She thanked the officer. Had this accident been so well planned that it was to make it look like an accident whereby her husband died? Maybe he needed to disappear?

Lucy made herself a simple meal that night and she had a glass of wine with it. When she had finished eating she went into the lounge with her glass and looked for something on the TV she could lose herself in, a film or programme she did not mind. She found a film, a romcom, great to unwind to, so she settled herself in for the night. She must have dropped off to sleep while watching it as she suddenly jumped, waking herself up from a dream where she was about to fall off the edge of the building. She caught her breath and then orientated herself in the room and realised where she was. She looked at the clock. It was late, she needed to go to bed now. She switched the TV off and went to bed.

The next morning she woke at eight and felt refreshed; no more bad dreams thank goodness. They unnerved her. She showered, dressed and went down for breakfast. She had just finished when a knock at the door came. She went to see who it was and the delivery guy stood there with a secure parcel that needed her signature. She signed and took it into the house. Carefully she unwrapped it and found a box inside which when she opened it made her gasp. It was the diamond bracelet that Alex had wanted to buy for her in Mayburn at the jewellers, he must have gone back to buy it for her. She noticed a note inside the box. She carefully pulled it out and read it 'Will love you always, Alex'. A tear trickled down her cheek. She was not sure whether it was sorrow or happiness but the tears flowed. After a while she composed herself and thought, had he been alive when he sent it or did it mean he was still alive?

She picked up the phone and dialled Dean, she needed to speak to someone. He was the only one she could confide in. The phone rang and was diverted to his assistant as he was with clients and would not be free until lunchtime. She did not want to leave her name, so it would have to wait, and she would try ringing him later after she had been to the bank in Mayburn. She would also pop into the jewellers as well while she was in the village.

She parked her car and walked over to the bank. She spoke to the assistant she had spoken to before and showed her the documents she needed to see to allow her access to the safety deposit box. The assistant showed her to an office and sent for the box. It did not take much time and someone brought it in and put it on the desk. The assistant asked if she had a key and Lucy replied, "It's a bit embarrassing as I found two and I'm not sure which one will fit this box."

The assistant said, "Don't worry we come across this all the time when someone dies and leaves keys. Relatives are not sure what they are opening."

Lucy said, "Here you can try both and see which works."

The assistant took the two keys from her and first tried the one that was on a pretty key fob but would not go in, so then tried the other key. It went into the lock and turned it. Click, it was unlocked. Knowing it had opened it the assistant left her to explore the box on her own. She opened the box and found a letter addressed to Lucy. She opened the letter. She quietly read it....

My Darling Lucy,

If you are reading this I must be dead. I would like to thank you for the short time we have known each other and say that I loved your vibrant personality, your smile, your compassion and everything else about you that attracted me to you. I will miss you with all my heart and love you always.

I hope now you will accept the present of the bracelet with all my love.

Alex xxx

Lucy looked up from reading it, tears flowing down her face. Was that really him she buried, she was now starting to believe that it could be him. She turned it over. It was another letter, she read it .....

Lucy my dear,

If you are reading this side, I hope I can explain more. I have not been fully honest with you and I apologise for that. It is hard for me as I did not expect to fall in love with you so quickly like I did. It complicated matters. I hope you will accept the situation and carry on with your life and find love again. You have my blessings on that.

The key to things may not be for studying but you may want to sleep on it or keep it under wraps

Love you always, Alex xxx

Lucy sobbed. What does it mean, had she lost him forever? The last paragraph was meaningless she thought. She put the letters in her bag, wiped her eyes and closed the box, now empty and relocked it. She pressed the intercom and someone answered. She said she was finished and a few minutes later the assistant came back to the room. After thanking her for her help she left the bank and headed straight across the road to the jewellers.

She pushed the door and entered the shop and went up to the counter and asked to see the manager. She waited for a few minutes and he came out and introduced himself as the manager and asked how could he help her. She asked, "I came into this shop a few months ago with my husband and we looked at a diamond bracelet but changed my mind and did not buy it."

He nodded and said, "Yes the gentleman came back and bought it on the understanding that I would hold it safely until I was contacted by a firm of Funeral Directors telling me of his demise. I thought it was a strange request at the time but agreed with the arrangements."

She said, "That was my husband who bought the bracelet."

He said, "I am so sorry to hear of your loss but did the bracelet arrive safely?"

"Yes it arrived safely and it was a shock to see it again."

She thanked him again and left the shop and headed to the car park. She drove home with a mind on lots of things but one thing was sure, she need to speak to Dean and get him round to talk about what she had found so far, and what that last sentence meant in the letter. Maybe she would sleep on it first.

Chapter 4

She woke the next day and decided that she needed to share the letters with Dean especially the last paragraph, as it was bothering her. It was the weekend tomorrow so maybe they could meet up for lunch.

She rang his office and got straight through on his direct line. He apologised for not ringing her yesterday as the meeting ran over and then he was late for the next meeting. He knew she had rung as the assistant had recognised her and mentioned that she had rung but not left a message. He hoped they could catch up over the weekend and Lucy said what about lunch tomorrow which he agreed to. He mentioned he knew a nice quiet place where they could go and talk over lunch. She offered to pick him up but he insisted that he would pick her up about eleven. It was all arranged and she said good bye to him and put the phone down.

Lucy sat in the kitchen nursing a cup of coffee looking at the letters she had found yesterday. Who was this man she married who loved her so much? She opened the letters that she had found yesterday and read them again. What should she do? She was unsure, maybe Dean would be able to make some sense about everything.

She got up from the table and went into the study where she felt close to Alex with all his favourite books which he used to read in there. She stretched out on the chaise longue like Alex did when he was reading his books. She loved the chaise longue, she had bought it for the study and had re-upholstered it to match the décor. She had picked up a book from the table - whether she or Alex had left it she was not sure. She put her feet up and opened the book. Yes, it was hers, a silly romantic novel which Alex would pull her leg about. She started to read it but it was not long after that she felt sleepy and was soon asleep.

She was woken suddenly by the ringing of the phone. She went over then picked it up only to be surprised to hear her sister on the other end. She was concerned that Lucy might not be coping with everything but she reassured her she was doing fine. After putting her mind at ease she put the phone down and looked at her watch to see what time it was, as she was not sure how long she had been to sleep. It was six thirty and she was feeling hungry now, so headed to the kitchen to make her-self something quick and simple.

She looked in the fridge and decided to pan fry some chicken with salad, and she had some nice bread she could warm up as well. It was soon done and she was sitting down eating it not realising how hungry she was. After she had finished eating and clearing up she went into the lounge to watch some TV. She went to pour herself a drink from the cabinet, Alex loved his whiskey but she drank anything. She knew she would have to stop feeling sorry for herself as she sat down with her drink watching TV alone.

The next morning after a good sleep with no nightmares she felt rested. She got herself ready for when Dean was calling to pick her up. She picked the letters up and put them into her bag. He arrived on time and she locked up the house and got into his car. They chatted about everything, hobbies, work and travel as they drove and before they knew it they had arrived at the restaurant. It looked charming and they parked the car and went in. It was not very busy and they got a table tucked away in the corner and ordered some soft drinks. The waiter brought the menus and specials and both looked at the menu and decided what they wanted to order. While waiting for their order to be taken they started talking about the letters. The waiter came and took the order.

Lucy pulled the envelope out of her bag saying to Dean, "This is what I found in the safety deposit box in the bank. They are very personal to me but I still want you to read them."

Dean hesitated, "Are you sure you want me to read them?"

"Yes," and she pushed it forward to him. He read the first one and then she said he must read the second one on the back, as well. After reading the second one he sat back in his chair thinking for a while before he spoke. "Lucy do you think he is dead or alive?"

She knew in her heart the man she buried was not her husband as he would not have been stupid enough not to wear a seat belt. The only explanation was that someone else was involved and the car had been tampered with.

Lucy spoke, "It is hard to decide and I am not sure of the last paragraph on the second letter whether that's Alex being funny."

Dean replied, "So are you saying gut instinct says he is alive but doesn't want to be found?"

She nodded and took a sip of her drink. Did she realise what she just said and was she willing to look further for clues? They talked a little more before the food came.

They enjoyed the meal and did not discuss the letters anymore till after they finished. Both had a chance to mull over things in their minds, where to go from here. Dean spoke first, "Well I would say it is fool hardy for you to put yourself at risk by looking any further. Accept you buried him and move on with your life. You may not like what you find out if you don't and then you can't go back."

Lucy looked surprised or was he trying to protect her from the evil she may uncover if she looks further? Lucy then said, "What about the paragraph?"

He said, "There has to be more in the study you have not found and if you want to go further I will support you as much as I can on the understanding that if it gets too dangerous for either of us we drop this like a hot stone." She nodded to agree with what he had just said.

They decided that after they had paid the bill they would head back to her house and start the search in the study for clues looking at all the books. They arrived at the house and went through the front door. Before they started they wanted a coffee so went into the kitchen to get one each.

They then went into the study to start looking. They had one key left to fit some lock. They both started looking at the books on the book case, picking them up one at a time and flicking through the pages in case something was inside the book. This was going to take some time. Lucy was putting the books back on the shelf after they had looked at them. Suddenly a little piece of paper fluttered from one of the books pages that Dean had opened. Lucy picked it up. It was actually a photograph of her and Alex when they first met, but why had he put it in a book? She looked at the name of the book but it did not ring any bells with her, so put the book and photo to one side. They kept going until they decided to have a break and both sat on the chaise lounge when an idea came to her.

"You may want to sleep on it and keep it under wraps", she said and Dean turned to her wondering what she meant. She pointed to what they were sitting on and looked down at the rug underneath. Lucy asked Dean to move the rug and chaise lounge, and dropped down onto the floor looking for a loose floor board. She knocked them to see if they rattled and then Dean ended up joining her on the floor for her search. They must have looked silly, people who had lost their minds. After a few minutes Lucy said, "There is nothing here, we are wasting our time," and burst into tears.

Dean came over and put his arm around her. She pushed her face into his shoulder. He said, "Just let it go," she did, she sobbed and cried so much she was not sure where the sorrow came from. She lifted her tear stained face up and looked into his eyes, "I am sorry but I seemed to have made a rather wet mess on your shirt." They laughed and he said not to worry it would wash. He helped her up and gave her a hankie so she blew her nose and wiped her eyes.

"You need a cup of tea with a shot of something I think, I'll make it for you," he said.

She said, " Add some honey rum, it's better than sugar."

He went off to the kitchen while she composed herself again and then joined him in the kitchen where she sat down. He put the tea in front of her. "Are you sure you want to go on with this poking about into Alex's life or will you stop now?" Dean said looking at the state she was in at present. She didn't reply, only sipped the tea.

"It's your life but I don't want you throwing it away on chasing ghosts," he continued. She sipped more tea. What did she want to find out, she was unsure. Whether to confirm Alex was dead, disappeared off the face of the earth, she did not know. She was unsure at this moment in time and so she shrugged her shoulders at him as her reply.

Dean said they had done enough today and she looked drained. He started looking in her cupboards to see what was available for him to cook her some tea. She watched him as he opened the cupboards and then decided to direct him to the right ones, where the food was. It was a simple salad he made for her which when he put it front of her and by this time she had come around. Was it because he had taken over her kitchen and prepared this for her or coaxed her out of her shell when she had retreated?

He sat down with her at the table and as they ate she asked about his life and how he got where he was and the women he had met along the way. He said the ones he liked didn't want to settle down when he did. So he got to the stage where he had given up looking for a partner to settle down with.

After they had eaten, she looked tired so he decided to leave. They said their good byes with a hug and a kiss on her cheek and she thanked him. After he left she crawled into bed feeling drained and hoped for a good night's sleep and no more nightmares.

Chapter 5

The next morning she woke with a headache, took some tablets, and had a shower which made her feel a little bit better. She dressed and went downstairs to put some coffee on when her phone rang. It was Dean to see how she was and if she wanted him to drop some freshly baked goodies in on his way to work. He said he used a local shop he had dealt with that supplies the office, she could have her pick. It was tempting and she had not eaten yet. She said yes.

The doorbell rang five minutes later. She opened the door and there was Dean holding a basket of baked goodies. He told her to choose what she wanted and then he would take the rest into the office. He followed her into the kitchen so she could take what she wanted. She took three Danish pastries which she put on a plate. He asked if she was okay after yesterday and said she was getting there. He said he would leave her alone for a few days to see what she wanted to do next. She thanked him.

She shut the door. He was growing on her but what would she do if she found her husband? Time would tell. She needed to find out what the last key opened if anything. She would have to look at everything in the house that might have a lock.

Lucy sat down to her delicious Danish pastries along with a strong cup of coffee and pondered what to do next and which room to start in. After she had finished she decided to start looking in the kitchen. It was interesting what she found at the back of the cupboard and in the drawers. Things she had misplaced over the years were found. She found it therapeutic. So much so that at the end of the day she had re-organised everything and got rid of a lot of things she had not used for some time. She felt pleased with herself as she sat down to her meal. Looking on the down side, she found nothing that would unlock with the key. Never mind, more rooms to search in the coming days.

Dean phoned that evening. He was on his way home after a heavy day at the office. He asked how her day had gone and she explained what she had been up to. They chatted for a while and Dean said he would cook her a meal one evening if she liked at his place. She said that would be lovely and they agreed to do it in the next couple of days. She put the phone down. Was she doing the right thing chasing ghosts? She would sleep on it.

The next morning she woke with a start, she had been dreaming. It was about Alex this time. It was about the time he gave her a present of a fur wrap which she said was silly as she had nowhere to wear it. Then a week later they were invited to a posh dinner where she could actually wear the wrap with a wonderful dress she bought on the spur of the moment. He even organised a limo to take them to an exclusive restaurant.

She wondered what had happened to it as she could not recall seeing it and Alex had said he would find a place for it. She needed to search the wardrobes. She got up and put her dressing gown on to start the search of the wardrobes. She opened one lot of doors and looked at cupboards and shelves but nothing. Then she looked into the next one until she came to the last one. It was to top section where she saw the box and it all came back to her. She pulled it down and opened the box, yes it was her fur wrap. Then she looked back into the top section, it was a safe. When had Alex installed one? She did not know but maybe it would be opened with a key, the one she had left. When she looked closer it did not have a lock but a keypad. What number then would it be? Something that both of them knew, birthdays, anniversaries? She tried different combinations but nothing worked.

She needed to phone Dean to see if he had any ideas. She had to dress first, then going downstairs, she grabbed something off the fruit bowl and then the phone rang. It was Dean. He said, "My police friend just phoned, the car was registered to hire firm and it was a company that had hired it from the airport for an employee. He could not give me any more information otherwise he would be in trouble. We can assume therefore, that the guy at the cemetery was checking up on what they had heard."

Lucy said, "I would leave it for the moment." Then she told him the news about the safe she had found but could not find the combination to it. It went quiet. "Are you there Dean?"

"Sorry, yes just thinking about Alex's office as I told everyone I would sort his things out. Maybe I might come up with something, leave it with me." She said he could let her know when she comes round for the meal tomorrow night if he finds anything. He replied, "Yes not a problem, see you about seven okay." She agreed and put the phone down.

She felt disappointed as she thought he would have an answer. Never mind, she would go back to the bedroom to see if she could find any other clues in the drawers. She went upstairs and started looking but kept finding Alex's cuff links and tie pins but nothing that would give her a hint of numbers to use. She sighed and thought, why can't she get the answers she needs? She had to be patient.

She went down to the study and pulled the books to open the secret drawer that she had found. She took the books within the drawer out and hoped they might give her a clue to the numbers for the safe or was it a wild goose chase? She had to try.

Dean unlocked the door to Alex's office and walked in. It was fairly tidy as he said he was going away so did not want to leave files on his desk he assumed. Dean found a file out, on the desk with a note attached saying 'to be typed up'. He checked the drawers, only one was locked. He knew where the key was kept as Alex had told Dean about it a few months ago. He found the key and unlocked the drawer, pulled it open and saw a file. He picked it up and looked at the name but it didn't register with him at first. He opened the file and flicked through the pages. Normal company returns, a few off-shore accounts, so the company must have been dealing with large sums of money. He looked at the name again. Now it rang a bell. It was the same name the police came up with about the car, registered to the same company.

Dean closed the file and the drawer and took the file into his office for a more detailed look through. At first he could not see anything strange or out of the ordinary but then he started calculating the figures that were there. It was larger amounts than normal for fees charged which was usually left to the discretion of senior management. He picked up the phone. He needed information on Alex's bank account.

The phone rang and Lucy answered, surprised to hear from Dean but a pleasant surprise. He asked her to check Alex's bank statements for sums of money exceeding two thousand pounds every month over say the last year and a half. Lucy was curious but did not ask at this moment why. She said she would ring him back once she had found them in the study filed away and come back to him. Dean thanked her and put the phone down.

Dean went back to the file. Yes the company was the same as the guy who hired the car and was at the funeral. Was Alex involved with a company who was money laundering and got too close or did he do them a favour too many and they decided to get rid of him? Or did Alex fake his death to get away from them? Dean was unsure what to do next. He would see if anyone from this company Alex was dealing with contacted him as he was Alex's boss.

He went back into Alex's office to put the file back in the drawer when something caught his eye. A silver locket and chain must have been underneath the file. He picked it up, turning it in his hands, and opened it to find a picture of Alex and Lucy. Dean explored further by taking both pictures out and then saw numbers engraved underneath each picture. He put the pictures back carefully and snapped the locket shut and put it in his pocket. He would show Lucy tomorrow when he saw her. He put the file back in the drawer and locked it. The file on top of Alex's desk he picked up and took to the assistant to sort and type the necessary and to return the file to him when it had been done.

Dean went back to his office and went back to his work when his phone rang. It was Lucy, " Hi, I have found some old bank statements but they only go back six months. If you want more I will have to get in touch with the bank which will be a couple of days."

Dean said, "That's okay I can wait but did you

look at the figures on the statements?"

Lucy replied, "Yes, there seems to have been regular payments going in but increasing in amounts up to the last statement. The last sum was five thousand pounds. What was he doing with the money?"

Dean replied, "I am not sure." He went on to tell her about the file and possibly Alex was involved with money laundering, taking the money into his account and then passing it on to another account. It could be from drugs, gambling, anything to get rid of the money whatever way possible. He thanked her for her help and asked, "Would you like to come round tonight rather than tomorrow so we can discuss what we have so far?"

Lucy agreed, "That is a good idea, give me your address and I'll see you at seven."

He gave her his address and directions and said he would see her later. He put the phone down and decided in his mind what he would cook her, but needed to call at the supermarket on the way home from work.

The day went quickly for both of them. She changed and decided to take a photo of the safe to show him, what for she was not sure but she did it. She was looking forward to the meal and his company as she found him charming to be with. She jumped in the car and headed for his house.

She pulled up outside his house, parked and walked up to the door. She knocked and Dean opened it and invited her in. She noticed his hazel eyes for the first time. He was casually dressed in jeans and t-shirt with a shirt over the top. She noticed for the first time he was muscular, maybe he worked out in a gym? She moved into a room which was tastefully decorated, nothing too bright and in your face. He offered her a drink and said that would be fine, red wine, she thought she could always take a taxi home.

Lucy then said, "Something smells nice. Are you going to tell me what it is or do I have to wait and see?" Dean said she had to wait as they had a lot to talk about before dinner. She thought to herself looking at him properly for the first time, how handsome he looked. She smiled to herself but he said, "What's the problem?"

"Nothing, sorry, was distracted, go ahead and tell me your news."

Dean went on to tell her about the file that Alex had been working on and that it was connected to the company of the man they saw at the funeral, and how money had been changing hands into Alex's account, large sums that would be questionable. He said he would be interested when the payments into his account stopped. Dean then pulled out the locket he had found in the drawer with the file and handed it to Lucy. She turned it in her fingers and said, "I have not seen this for some time as it had disappeared from my trinket box."

Dean said, "Open it, and look at what I have found inside, not just your photos."

Lucy clicked it open and there were their pictures, then he instructed her to remove each one and look at the inside of the locket. Dean knew by her expression that the numbers were new and had not been there before.

Lucy pushed the locket into Dean's hands and said, "What do they mean, why would Alex have done that and keep it from me?"

Dean looked at the numbers, "Do you think he was heading for trouble and to cover his tracks put the numbers of the safe inside the locket to hide them? He maybe thought things had gone too far and saw no way out and then made it look like he died?"

Lucy swallowed hard, "I don't know but I will see if the numbers work either way and see what the safe is hiding, if anything."

Dean put the pictures back in the locket for Lucy and handed it back to her. She put it on. It felt safer that way. She didn't want to lose it again. A buzzer went off, the noise coming from the kitchen. Dean excused himself and went into the kitchen. Lucy touched the locket around her neck and thought to herself, did I really know you Alex with all this secrecy. She sighed to herself.

Dean popped his head around the kitchen doorway and asked her to join him in the kitchen. As she joined him in the kitchen, something smelt nice and enticing. He patted the kitchen stool for her to sit as he continued to get the vegetables ready. She looked around and found that the room was not just the kitchen but dining room as well as a sitting area. He asked her to go to the table as everything was ready now, so she picked up her glass and walked over to the table and settled down. He apologised for not making a starter but said there was a pudding to fill her up.

He brought the dishes to the table and offered to put food on her plate which she was quite happy for him to do, stopping him where necessary. She waited for him to serve himself and then she started to eat. The meat just melted in her mouth with the noodles and vegetables it was delicious. She was impressed with his cooking and said so too. They laughed when he said maybe they should open a restaurant together as they were both good cooks. He topped up her wine glass and they talked about his house and how long he had lived there and many more things were talked about. It was just small talk over a delicious meal.

They both finished and Dean cleared the dishes up and went to get the pudding for them. What he brought out was a banoffee pie, which impressed Lucy, but then he confessed he had not cooked it, but the girls at the bakery he used for the office had done it for him. She laughed and said it still looked good.

They both had a slice each and it was wonderful, but were both full and could not eat any more. Dean suggested, if she wanted he would call tomorrow evening and they could open the safe together and he would bring some of the leftover pie over as well. Only if she wanted him to, she just had to say.

"Of course, that would be great, thanks," she said. After moving to the comfy lounge they listened to music and drank some more wine. It was getting late now and she felt she needed to make a move to go.

Dean said, "You can stay the night in the spare room, if you think you are okay with me?" and he winked at her. She gave a nervous laugh. What would she do, did she have to go home? He was at work tomorrow so no lie in.

He said, "Don't worry, I do respect you and maybe it was foolish of me suggesting it. It did seem silly you getting a taxi when I had a spare room you could use. You would only have to come back in the morning to pick your car up as well."

She had to agree, he did talk sense, "Okay then I'll stay in the spare room. Thanks for your hospitality." He said he would lend her a shirt of his to sleep in and he always had spare tooth brushes as he did a lot of travelling with business. She accepted his kind offer and showed her to the room. It had its own ensuite as well. He brought her the shirt, towel, toothbrush and tooth paste for her. She turned and kissed him on the cheek, "Thanks for being such a good friend in a time of need." He just said he would see her in the morning and she shut her door. She did not realised how tired she was until her head touched the pillow. She was asleep in minutes.

Chapter 6

She woke with the sun streaming through the window. She felt slightly disorientated for a few moments until she remembered where she was and that she had actually stayed the night at Dean's. A knock on her bedroom door, "Are you decent?" Dean called out.

"Yes, I'm fine, come in," not expecting him to come in holding a tray with what looked like breakfast for her. She was taken aback by his kindness. He came in and put it on the bed.

"For me? Well I must come here more often with this service," she laughed.

Dean said, "Its only coffee, juice and toast."

She said, "And very nice too."

He said there were towels and shower stuff in the bathroom if she wanted to shower before she went, but she said she would leave as soon as she had eaten her breakfast and got dressed. He said that was not a problem and left the room, closing the door behind him.

Lucy ate her breakfast, made herself look as presentable as possible and went downstairs taking the tray with her. She told Dean that she would see him tonight for them to have a go at opening the safe between them and she would cook dinner for them.

Dean said, "That's a date, see you later." He showed her out of the house, she got into her car and headed home.

When she arrived she went straight upstairs to shower and change her clothes from last night. She felt better now. She needed to plan dinner for tonight so decided to go out to the supermarket. While she was out she called into the bakery Dean used to supply his company with morning danishes. She was chatting with the owner to see if there was a vacancy at all, either to train or volunteer in the preparation part of the bakery. She loved bread making and wanted to learn more. The owner said she would think about it and took her details.

Lucy continued shopping for her ingredients for the meal, remembering that Dean would be bringing pudding for them. When she got home she started preparing things ready to go into the oven when the time came. When everything was done and ready she went upstairs to change.

She walked into the bedroom and the fur wrap was still laid on the bed in the box. She picked the wrap up and noticed a piece of paper in the bottom of the box. Yes, she remembered, Alex had left her a note with the wrap and she had kept it. She wouldn't read it. Too many memories. She put the wrap back in the box on top of the note, put the lid on and decided to put the box elsewhere in the wardrobe for the time being.

She changed her clothes, did her hair and make-up and went downstairs. She put some music on, went into the kitchen, put her dish in the oven and poured herself a glass of her favourite red wine. She then went to sit down in the lounge and after a few minutes the door-bell rang. She went to the door and Dean was standing holding the box with the pudding in. She invited him in, taking the box off him at the same time. She took it into the kitchen and put it in the fridge for later. Then she picked up a glass and poured him some wine and took it to him in the lounge.

After she had given him the glass, she took the

locket off from around her neck and gave it to Dean in his unoccupied hand. He put his glass down and gently removed the photographs from either side of the locket and exposed the numbers engraved inside.

He said, "Show me the safe and we will give it a go with these numbers to see if it will open it."

Lucy led the way upstairs to her bedroom and into the walk-in wardrobe where the safe was and said, "You do it. Fingers crossed."

Dean tried the first set and then the handle but it didn't work. Then he reversed the sequence of figures and the handle gave this time and the door opened. Inside was a box. Dean took in out of the safe and noticing it needed a key to unlock it. Lucy went to the drawer in the bedside cabinet and pulled the last key she had found of Alex's. She gave it to Dean to try. He said, "Are you sure you want me to open this box? It could change everything."

She nodded, "Yes, please open it."

Dean put the key in and turned and opened the box and looked inside. He thought this does not look right. Inside he saw four passports. He removed them and started to open the first one. The picture was Alex but the name was different. In fact all four had different names and also Alex had a beard in some of the pictures as well. He handed them to Lucy.

Lucy looked up at Dean, "What does this mean?"

"I'm not sure, he may have had a double life or he was travelling under different names for the money laundering company which I found details of in his office," Dean said.

Lucy sat thumbing the passports, deep in thought, then handed them back to Dean asking him to put them back into the box and lock it and put it back in the safe. She did not know what to do now, he had warned her. They went downstairs. She needed a stronger drink than wine at this moment and headed for the kitchen. She took a bottle of vodka and poured a small glass and took a gulp of it when Dean walked in.

"Are you okay? Well actually you looked a bit shocked. Do you want to talk about it and get it off your chest?" Dean said.

Lucy turned to him and said, "Where do I start?" He motioned her to sit down on a stool in the kitchen and then she started and once she did it just flooded from her. What sort of man had she married, not who she thought, he was a stranger, all the deceit. She knew she had only known him for a few years but he had not been honest with her. Did he actually love her? She was questioning even that now.

Dean lifted her face and kissed her. She drew back. He said, "Sorry but I had to do something to stop you talking that way". Okay she thought, a surprise at the time, but nice that he cares. She smiled to herself that was nice. Should she say anything? No, but she apologised for having such a rant about Alex. She needed to get the food sorted for dinner now, so she stood up when he took hold of her shoulders and said, "We will find out what he was up to if you want but don't know how deep he was involved with things." She shrugged. She didn't know either at this moment in time. His hands dropped and she walked forward with him moving to one side as she headed for the cooker.

Dean changed the subject when they were both in the kitchen and talked about food and what was on the menu tonight. They settled down to their meal and a silence descended upon them as they ate. Then Dean broke the silence and said, "You know I have to do some investigation into this Company as it involved my business and Alex was dealing within its parameters and it is my Company's reputation I have to consider as well."

She acknowledged that and offered any help accessing Alex's bank details or anything else he needed. When they had finished Dean mentioned the desert that he had brought round and Lucy removed it from the fridge and put it on the table after clearing it and brought two bowls and a serving spoon. They both had some and it was so delicious it reminded her of her visit to the bakery.

"Dean I forgot to mention, I visited the bakery you go to and made enquiries about me helping and learning bread making especially," Lucy said.

Dean replied, "That's great, something to occupy yourself with, especially learning new skills."

"Yes I think it may be an opportunity for my food and cooking skills to be used in a good way and learn something along the way as well," she said.

Dean went on to say he thought that was definitely a step in the right direction. They had coffee in the kitchen rather than the lounge as Dean needed to leave shortly afterwards. They rose together and walked towards the door. He turned and gently kissed her on the lips and then left saying he would be in touch.

Lucy shut the door. She sighed and reflected on how things had developed with Dean. She hoped Dean would take charge of things if Alex had been involved with the Company he was working for.

Chapter 7

Dean arrived at work the next day and decided to contact his police friend to see if he could put him in touch with a colleague on the matter of money laundering. He knew under the Money Laundering Regulations 2007 he had to report anything, and this Company Alex was dealing with looked all wrong from the paperwork he had looked at. He needed professional advice on what to do next.

Dean rang his friend, explained the situation he was in. It all pointed to the man that hired the car who was seen at the funeral. Was he connected to the same Company Alex was dealing with? He told Dean that someone would be in contact with him sometime today. Dean thanked him.

Dean put the phone down and went into Alex's office and retrieved the file and sat down at his desk and started to study it in more detail, making notes as he did. Discrepancies appeared that he could not find an answer to. The deeper he looked Alex appeared to have manipulated the figures to add up on the balance sheets and the profit and loss part of the accounts. He was good at his Job.

It was about an hour later that the phone rang. It was a gentleman called Neil, and he asked how he could assist Dean. So Dean went over the details he had assembled so far and told Neil that he believed Alex, who was now dead, was involved in money laundering or fraud. At this stage he was not sure which. It was too complicated to discuss fully over the phone, and was not sure who to go to with what he had found.

Neil suggested that an informal meeting over

coffee would be a good start just in case things were still live and they might contact his company as he was the other partner in the firm. Dean agreed and suggested a venue. Tomorrow morning was good for both of them. Dean thanked him and put the phone down. He felt a little better but still did not know where things stood.

He continued with the file and rang certain departments for information appertaining to the Company Alex was dealing with. He needed to know how long this had been going on, and had Alex been filing false tax forms as well. By the end of the day a picture was unfolding and not a good one either.

Dean was thinking of ringing Lucy to tell her he had made contact with the Metropolitan Police, but decided against it just yet. He needed to speak to Neil first. He locked the papers in his drawer and left for the day.

He did not sleep very well that night, tossing and turning in bed, feeling guilty that he had not recognised things were different with Alex or why he had not asked for help sooner. Was it because he had dug himself in too deep in the matter and therefore he did not want to involve anyone else? If he had asked for help maybe it would have stopped him being killed.

The next morning, feeling tired from lack of sleep, Dean went to the coffee shop he had told Neil to meet him at, and said which booth he would be in. Neil arrived but Dean was surprised by his appearance, in a suit holding a briefcase with him. They shook hands and sat down in the booth that was tucked away in the corner, looking like two business men having a meeting.

Neil said, "I have to be honest with you we knew

partly about what was going on with Alex, and he was concerned for his life. He thought once he had a full dossier on the Company he would let us go in. Sadly that did not happen and we still have missing bits to be able to make a case to allow us to raid the Company and take them to court."

Dean leaned back, feeling shocked and sorry for Lucy, as he now realised it was Alex in the car crash after all. Could this Company have tampered with the car as well? He would have to be sure before he told her or maybe Neil should be the one.

Dean said, "Well the problem is I have lots of questions but this is not the place. It is too public."

Pulling a card from his wallet Dean said, "Book yourself an appointment to see me at the office next week, and by that time I will have collected all that is available about the case so far, and you can take it from there."

Neil said, "Thanks I'll do that," taking his card out but writing on the back 'ring if you need me before for anything' and then gave Dean the card.

They stood up and shook hands. Dean paid for his coffee and they left together, but both walking off in opposite directions. Dean went back to the office and rang Lucy. He needed the bank statements from her and the multiple passports that they had found as well. He was forgetting the code books and weapons they had found, but he felt they could wait to be dealt with. He decided at this moment in time not to mention Neil, just that he needed the details to put in the file.

He dialled her number. It was ringing and she answered. He enquired how she was and then asked her about the bank statements. "Do you have the ones you found and also the ones you requested yet?"

Lucy had answered that she had now got all the statements he had asked for from the bank and what would he like her to do with them. He asked if she had time to drop them off at his office, as he was working on the figures in the file and that would assist him to clarify things. She agreed that she would be at the office in about an hour to drop them off. He thanked her and she put the phone down.

She went into the study to collect everything together. Finding an envelope big enough in the stationery drawer, she put them in and sealed it. She had time for a quick coffee before she left for his office, as it would not take her long because the traffic was light. After her coffee, she picked up the envelope - too big to go in her handbag, and walked out of the door.

She parked the car in the office car park and walked into the entrance, and to the lift. She waited and then entered the lift. His office was on the sixth floor. The doors opened, and she exited the lift and went to reception. The receptionist recognised her from the funeral and asked was she doing okay and how could she help her. Lucy said she was here to see Dean. The receptionist buzzed his office and he told her to show Lucy through to his office. They walked together and then the door was opened for her, and Lucy entered Dean's office. He stood up, offered her a chair, and shut the door. Lucy put the envelope on his desk. He opened it and took the statements out.

Dean skimmed the statements. Lucy said, "I have highlighted the abnormal amounts shown going in and out of the account which would not normally be there."

She also went on to say she had enquired at the bank about accounts that Alex had. Now she was involved with dealing with his estate, and could access the money, but did not want to touch it at this stage of the proceedings. She had told the bank about Dean and that she would give him authority to investigate the accounts accordingly. Dean rang for his assistant to bring in a form for Lucy to sign confirming this. A knock at his door and she entered to give him the form and he thanked her. Dean filled in the necessary details and got Lucy to sign it and fill in her bit as well. He would email that form to her solicitor just to keep paperwork correct.

Lucy thanked him. Dean said, "Just a minute I need something else from you. The code books and passports I think would be safer out of the house and put in my safe here." He went on to say, "The weapons we will have to take advice on from the police in case Alex didn't have a license."

Lucy said, "Okay but I don't want a fuss with police cars outside my house." Dean agreed and said he would try and get it done discreetly for her.

Dean said, "Can I call on my way to work in the morning at about ten if that's not too early for you?"

She nodded and then stood up. He came round from behind the desk towards her and held her in an embrace with her saying, "It will work out and we will discover exactly what has been going on, won't we?"

He released her from the embrace, and looked into her eyes and said, "I hope we do."

He went and opened the door for her. She followed him and walked out of the office then out of the building heading for her car. She drove home thinking that Dean was protecting her from the truth. Had Alex been on the take, or was he just doing an investigation on his own and stumbled upon the anomalies he found within his work. But why was he killed? She had to be patient and maybe Dean would eventually tell her the truth. She could be strong.

That evening she felt very alone, lost in a mist of where this was going. She could not concentrate on anything on the TV so decided to go to bed early. She was woken by nightmares about Alex which left her sweating and shaking in bed. Sleep was not easy that night and before she knew it the alarm went off. She hoped by jumping into the shower it would wake her up. She dressed and went downstairs to the study where she had left the passports and code books they had found, put them in an envelope, sealed it and took it with her to the lounge, ready to give to Dean when he called this morning. She walked into the kitchen and made herself a coffee and sat down not knowing whether she wanted breakfast this morning.

The doorbell rang. She went to answer it and opened the door and there Dean stood. He looked delicious standing there in his dark suit, so handsome. She smiled to herself and thought, no too soon after losing Alex, he is a friend which was what she needed right now, but who cared. Dean smiled, "Penny for your thoughts?"

That made Lucy check herself had it shown in her face? "Oh you're early."

Dean looked at his watch, "By about three minutes. Sorry, shall I go away and come back on time?"

Lucy smiled, "Sorry, do come in. The envelope is in the lounge. I'll go and get it but come in and shut the door."

She offered him a coffee as they went into the lounge together for the envelope. She picked it up and assured him the code books and passports that he asked for were in it and they went back to the front door with her opening it for him. He said, "Don't worry too much. I will be in touch once I have more to tell you." He leaned over and kissed her, taking her by surprise. He left and she closed the door behind him, thinking, that was nice.

When Dean arrived at the office he told his assistant that he had an important new client coming. Neil and he did not want to be disturbed for several hours and she was to hold all his calls and lay on some refreshments in his office. She went ahead and arranged it all for him. Half an hour later Neil arrived and was shown into Dean's office. They shook hands and he offered him a coffee to start with. They both had a coffee and settled down to the business in hand.

Dean handed over the file of statements to Neil for him to look over. He took his time making one word comments as he read. When he had digested it Dean handed him the envelope with the passports and code books. He opened it, and looked inside, and shut it and turned to Dean, "You start talking and I will fill in the gaps along the way," Neil said.

Dean said it was a bit sketchy at first but found that Alex had been approached over a year ago to work on the accounts of this Company. It looked legit at the time, and presumed they wanted to test Alex to see if he was the right guy to deal with things. It looked from the bank statement that they were paying him small amounts of money at first. Whether this was to buy assets for them or just to move the money around into off shore accounts or something else, he was not sure. Dean said Alex would go away for a few days here and there so nothing indicated he was moving money both in the bank and in suitcases for them. It was only when he died and Dean looked into the file did it start to unravel. Dean went on to say that when Alex's widow got in touch with him to say he had been killed in a car accident but was supposed to be in Paris, or that is what he told him, he was taken aback with things as they came to light. Alex's wife then came across strange things in the house she was not aware of, and started involving me as a friend and colleague/partner at work. She did doubt that it was Alex she was burying at one time and that he had faked his death. Then the stranger at the funeral made them both think something they did not understand was going on.

Neil was making notes as Dean was telling his tale so far and then looked up from his note book and said, "Is that it?"

Dean replied, "Yes, more or less, except that Lucy found weapons she did not know existed in the house, hidden away in a secret draw. She would like them removed but it needed to be done discreetly, with no police car present outside her door."

Neil made a note of that then started filling in the details. Alex was working undercover for the police, but was an actual accountant. He was recruited basically for this type of work, money laundering as it is big business and can also be linked with drugs. He was working fine for them when he fell for Lucy and although they were not too happy but Alex had said he could keep everything from her. Of course he met up with you and joined as a partner, which again gave him access to numerous companies of which the majority were above board until this job came along.

Alex was good at the cloak and dagger stuff and would disappear off the radar for days and they would be concerned he was in too deep instead of sharing information for them to help. The amount of information he had given so far and what they had collect previous to Alex's death would give them a good case and hopefully catch them before they disappeared.

Neil went on to say that he was sorry that he did not foresee the killing of Alex. He thought he was too valuable to them, but all he could say is it could be that he slipped up somewhere along the line, making them jumpy. Therefore they tampered with the car and killed him. Neil thought that it would be a good idea to copy all the files and for Dean to keep the originals. They might want to contact him in the future for further questions.

Neil also said that Dean's office had been under surveillance since his death in case the office was broken into. Dean nodded, and excused himself to copy the documents as he did not want to share the information with anybody else in the office. He was gone about ten minutes and when he returned he handed Neil the documents in a closed folder and put originals back in his file.

Dean asked, "What now?"

Neil replied, "We will use the information you have given us and hopefully take the case forward and we will arrange for someone, undercover, to call at Lucy's house to collect the weapons and dispose of them. That will be tomorrow afternoon. If you could inform her that would be great, thanks."

Dean nodded that he would do that. They both stood up. Dean shook Neil's hand and thanked him again, and showed him out of the office. When he had gone, Dean picked the file up and took it back to Alex's office to lock it in his drawer. When he left the office he decided he needed to speak to Lucy to tell her about everything now the police were dealing with it.

She answered the door, looking surprised to see Dean. Dean said, "Have you got a minute? I need to tell you something."

She let him in and led him through to the lounge. They both stood while Dean told her some news. He said an undercover policeman with a van would be calling tomorrow afternoon to pick up the weapons and dispose of them for her. She nodded, feeling nervous at what might come next. He said that he was not prepared to tell her everything, as Alex tried hard enough himself, when he was alive to protect her. He confirmed that it was Alex who she really buried.

"It was an accident let's say that should not have happened." She felt a little faint, and as her knees gave way Dean caught her and carried her to the settee. He lay her down until she regained consciousness.

She said, "Maybe it was me wishing it was not Alex in the car as I did not want to lose him."

Dean replied, "You could be right, but please don't blame him or yourself for what has happened."

Lucy went on to say, "Okay, I promise I will not blame myself as it was out of my control. Please can I have a glass of water from the kitchen."

Dean went into the kitchen and brought her back a glass of water which she sipped and then patted the settee next to herself for him to sit down.

She turned to him and said, "Thank you for being there for me, you don't know how much help it has been." She kissed him on the lips as to say thanks. He held her for a few seconds and then she pulled away.

"You have been through a lot lately. It is time for me to step back a little don't you think? I will always be available for you to phone me though," he said, and stood up saying, "I'll show myself out, just stay sat."

He left and closed the door behind him. She sat back on the settee feeling drained, and wondered if he would ever be back in touch with her in the future.

Chapter 8

The next afternoon Lucy waited for the van from the police to arrive, but not knowing what time they were due, was reluctant to get the weapons out of the drawer. She was in the kitchen reading the paper with a cup of coffee when the doorbell rang. She got up and answered it. Two gentlemen smartly dressed plus another gentleman who introduced himself as Neil, stood there with a small van parked on the drive, one of them had a large bag in one hand. They introduced themselves and showed her their police cards which stated they were from firearms sections.

She brought them into the house and asked for them to follow her to the study. They followed her. She asked them to put the bag on the desk. Then she opened the secret drawer by pulling at the books which opened it. The police officers took all the knives and guns that were in the drawer, wrote a receipt and listed the items, giving Lucy her copy and then they zipped the bag up. They left, leaving Neil behind to talk to Lucy.

Neil turned at the door and said to Lucy, "I'm sorry it has turned out this way with Alex. He was a valuable colleague." Lucy nodded and shut the door behind him. She just wanted to draw a line under things and put an end to this sham of life with Alex. The last three years -what were they for she asked herself. Okay she loved him but that's when the tears started to flow, he did mean a lot to her even though it was a short space of time. She had a good cry and felt better for it.

She now had to think about her life and move on to what she would do next. She had forgotten the job at the bakery. They said they would do a trial session to see how she got on, so there was something to look forward to as she loved food and so she should fit in nicely.

She slept soundly that night, at peace with herself now. She knew in the near future somehow everything would turn out right but there were still things to sort with the solicitor. Time would tell.

The next morning she turned up at the bakery nice and early; she was eager to learn. She loved the smell and getting her hands into the dough, kneading it, which she found was very therapeutic as well. She fitted in well at the bakery and after a couple of mornings there was offered to be shown how to do pastries. This was just what she needed, a challenge. She could see a future here.

Dean in the meantime was trying to deal with the work Alex had been involved with, to make sure he had given everything to Neil, but also Alex had other clients. Dean needed to reassure them that the service would continue until he got around to getting another partner for the firm. Dean only hoped that Neil would have enough evidence to take the Company to court and seize assets. He also wondered if they would ever find the person who tampered with Alex's car. He hoped that Alex's death was not in vain.

Thinking of Alex made his mind think of Lucy again. If it had been under different circumstances he would have persuaded her to come out on a date, but seeing she had not rung him probably he was reading her wrong. Maybe he reminded her of Alex and it was too much.

Dean thought he would ring her in a couple of months to see how she was. He drank his coffee at his desk and wondered if he would ever hear back from

Neil. Probably if it went to court, he might be called as a witness. He opened a file and stated working on some accounts.

Lucy, after a few months had passed, had settled the estate, and all the details were now sorted. She was enjoying being at the bakery, and one morning after she had been working making the daily bread, was asked to help in the shop as they were shorthanded.

She had just served someone and had her back to the counter when someone came in the door. She turned and there he stood, his dark eyes, that handsome smile, Dean. He was as surprised as she was to see her standing behind the counter.

He said, "Fancy seeing you here, I've come for our regular order for the office."

Lucy replied, "That's fine, I'll put the order together for you in the basket, if that's okay with you."

Dean replied, "That's great. It gives me a chance to see how you are."

They talked while she put the order into the basket which he collected every morning for the office. She told him that all the estate had now been settled, and he said he was starting to look for another partner, as he could not manage the work load on his own. She put the basket on the counter and passed it to him. As she did he caught hold of her hand. She looked up deep into his eyes.

He said, "How about I take you out for dinner tonight? Pick you up about seven?"

Lucy smiled at him, "You took your time asking me."

At which they both laughed!

GREEN WITH ENVY

Chapter 1

The house was draining their money. They needed to do something about it but it was hard to persuade him to look for another job. He was always in the garden. It was his life, he had such green fingers. Everything he touched would grow, even the plants that were struggling he breathed life into them. It was amazing what he did with the cuttings and plants. He was a miracle worker, green fingers and more. It was his passion and he was always talking to the plants. He would shut up when she walked into the greenhouse. He would look up and smile at her. He needed to find a job to feed his passion.

It was that smile that attracted her to him all those years ago and of course he was very handsome in his youth. He would say that he was not and disagree but when she looked at photographs, yes he was.

They met at a local dance, both being brought up in a rural area where they would have dances on a Saturday night at the local village hall. A bit old fashioned, but it was a long time ago when that sort of thing happened. They came from similar backgrounds and were able to talk about lots of things. They had a lot in common with each other. They would go on long walks together as they both enjoyed nature.

The only stumbling block was their parents. They were against them from marrying as they felt they were too young. The parents agreed for them to continue to see each other until he was due to go off to horticultural college and she would go off to teacher training college. They picked colleges so that they were not too far from each other and therefore continued to see each other. Over the years they built up a good relationship and they were certain they wanted to get married. The parents said they both needed to finish their courses, then if they still felt the same they agreed they could get married.

They knew in their heart of hearts they were made for each other, but only time would tell at the end of the courses each were doing. They finished, and both feeling the same towards each other, got married in the village where they had both been brought up. It was a wonderful day for the families and for them.

Janice and Harry, when married both looked for jobs and somewhere to live. They found jobs not far from each other and found a house to rent in a village not too far from where they worked.

Harry was lucky to find a job at a local National Trust house with formal gardens. He would have to help with seedlings/saplings in the greenhouse and nursery. He had people he was working with who had been gardeners for many years and therefore was hoping to gain experience from them as he worked.

Janice found a job in the village school teaching. It was lovely to feel part of the village life. She got to know all the children and families in the village as there was only a small amount of children attending the school. She was involved in the fetes that were arranged, in fact anything to help the village. It was an idyllic life and one they may one day look back on with fond memories.

Then Janice became pregnant. It was a shock to find it was twins, as they had no family history of twins. At first they could not tell and the doctors said one could have hidden behind the other, but they accepted that they had two babies coming not one. Her pregnancy went to plan and she gave birth to two healthy boys and welcomed them into the family.

Life was great for them. She had given up work to look after the babies rather than go back to work. Then a job of a life-time came up for Harry. It was at a large estate with a Manor house that needed a full time gardener plus handyman but accommodation came with the job. He jumped at the chance, in fact he decided to go for it without considering Janice and the children. It was only when he was offered the job he told her about it and that he was going to take the job. She could come and live with him in the accommodation offered with the job with the children. They would have the run of the grounds but not be allowed in the main house as the accommodation was a cottage on the estate. Or they could live separate lives where he would live away from home and see her and the children probably every weekend at the rented house. She was shocked at this. She thought the marriage was a case of sharing, give and take, but she was seeing another side of the man she agreed to spend the rest of her life with.

She felt he was selfish in deciding what he wanted but then she looked at it rationally after the dust had settled. Maybe it would be a chance of freedom for the children to have a safe environment to grow up in. It could work out to their advantage and not an opportunity to turn down too quickly. She wondered what the people were like who were employing her husband.

She agreed to move but needed to meet the owners of the house and said that she would take the children who were now three and loved being out of doors as much as possible with them. She needed to see if there would be no problems having children about.

Janice was nervous on the day of the visit and the

boys were excited and were smartly dressed. The owners of the Manor House, Mr & Mrs Giles, had told Harry to come and have tea and scones after they had looked at the cottage that went with the job. Janice had made a list of questions she felt she needed to ask them. They all climbed into the car, Janice strapping the excited twins into their seats, and she getting into the front seat.

Janice turned to Harry and said, "I'm nervous, do you think they will still offer you the job once they see me and the boys?"

Harry laughed, "Don't be silly they will love you like I do and especially the boys."

She shut the door of the car and they drove off.

Chapter 2

It was about a two hour drive deep into the countryside, passing fields of golden corn rippling in the summer sun. They travelled through picturesque villages with colourful displays of flowers. It was wonderful. They went through the nearest village to the estate and Harry pointed out the village school where the boys would go, and the post office that doubled as the village shop. Then there was the local public house. Harry drove on hoping in his heart that she would accept everything, as he had set his heart on the job.

He turned up the long drive towards the manor house, with trees and shrubs either side until it opened out and they could see the house. Janice said, "This is beautiful."

He said, "The cottage is not so grand. It might need a women's touch but soon you will see for yourself."

They pulled up in front of the manor house and Mr & Mrs Giles come through the front door to greet them as they pulled up. Janice thought they were middle aged and found out later they had no children or family alive. Harry opened his door and came round to meet them and shake hands then introduced his wife and the children. They made a fuss over the children which made Janice smile to herself. They were shown into the house and guided to the drawing room where tea was laid out for them.

Upon seeing the room Janice was very careful to make sure the children sat down and behaved themselves. The room was lavishly decorated and had a huge fireplace. Mr & Mrs Giles, Mary and William offered them a seat separate to the boys and had laid food out for the boys especially. The adults had different food. Mary explained they had a housekeeper who had lots of grandchildren and was used to making party food for them. So they decided to ask her to do something special for the boys coming. She hoped they would enjoy it. By the looks on their faces Janice was sure they would.

There were pinwheel sandwiches, fairy cakes with faces and animal biscuits. She was sure they would enjoy every mouthful. There was drink as well, she was glad she had brought their drinking cups with her. She filled them up for them and got them organised so they could start eating.

Janice turned to Mary to thank her and she said, "As long as the boys are happy it's fine." Mary then poured tea for them and started asking Janice about herself and then about the boys. There were scones and sandwiches for the adults as well to tuck into. It all looked delicious. William talked to Harry about the garden about what he wanted doing and his plan for the future. It would be hard work to begin with laying down the new garden. Harry turned to look at Janice to catch her eye, those beautiful green eyes. Yes the smile was there and she was taken by the family, he could see.

The boys were very content until one of them asked if they could go outside to play. Janice turned to Mary and was about to speak when Mary said, "Don't worry they can go out and play on the lawn. It is quite safe and there is a surprise for them as well." Mary stood up to open the French doors. The boys stood hesitantly and encouraged by their mum went with Mary outside to hear their voices shout with excitement when they spotted the tractors waiting for them. There were two small tractors with pedals. Harry went and joined them outside as Mary came back in. Janice said, "Thank you so much but you shouldn't have bought them for them."

Mary explained, "Oh don't worry they are hand me downs from my housekeeper, as I said she has a lot of grandchildren and they grow out of things so quickly."

Janice thanked her again. They both turned to look outside as the children shouting with joy and looked so excited with the tractors. Mary said to Janice, "I think we will leave them to it while we have a chat."

They both sat down. Mary topped up their cups with tea and then they talked, making Janice feel she was accepted into the house. She asked her all sorts of questions and while they were talking heard shrieks of delight from the children outside making both of them smile. Janice said she was concerned for the children straying onto the land surrounding the house and where was the cottage in relation to the house where they would live. Mary said it would not be a problem, stood up and went over to the French doors which she stuck her head through to tell her husband she was taking Janice to see the cottage. Both men said they would be fine with the boys and Mary shut the French doors. Janice followed her through the kitchen of the house, picked up the keys and encouraged Janice to follow her out of the door towards the cottage.

Janice noticed the size of the farmhouse kitchen she passed through to the door with the Aga cooker, lots of space to work and lots of cupboards for storage. A large table and chairs were in the middle of the floor and she noticed up against one wall a battered old settee and next to it a box of toys at the side. Janice pointed to the box and said to Mary, "I thought you didn't have children?"

"No they are for visiting children, actually the housekeeper, Betty's grandchildren," she said and then went on to say her children would be welcome to play with them as well if they called in.

Mary picked the keys up from a large dish with an assortment of keys in it. They were on a small wooden carved key ring. It said Rose Cottage on it. They walked out of the door and turned right, passed the triple garage and down the pathway under the arms of the trees tall and straight. They look as if they were planted a long time ago. They came into an open area when the sweet smell of roses reached her nose. She had not smelt anything like it ever. She could now see the cottage ahead of her and realised where the smell was coming from. It had double bay windows with a rambling rose either side of the door and a garden full of roses at the front. They walked down the path towards the door and the smell of the roses was so intense she said to Mary, "These roses are so perfumed they are beautiful."

Mary told her they were a very old variety, not like the new hybrid ones you get nowadays, which came from the main gardens of the house.

Mary put the key in the door of the cottage. Janice held her breath, not knowing what to expect, imagining cobwebs and dust everywhere with paper peeling. She was not looking forward to looking inside the cottage. Mary turned the key and pushed the door open. Janice's expression must have changed, which Mary noticed, as the door was pushed open and they both stepped inside. It was clean and airy and the sun was shining through the windows.

Janice's heart lifted and a smile appeared on her face.

There was a small hallway with doors to two rooms either side at the front with fireplaces in each of the rooms, but it had modern fires standing in the hearths. Mary pointed to the fire and said "They are electric and could be removed if you wanted a real fire, as the chimney has been swept in both rooms." Janice smiled.

They moved towards the back of the cottage, passing the staircase and downstairs toilet. Handy for the boys, she thought to herself. Mary opened the door into the kitchen/dining area which was large but cosy at the same time. Janice was over the moon so far with the downstairs but Janice held back her emotions not to show Mary how pleased she was so far. She just nodded. Mary then took her upstairs and showed her three bedrooms, one with an ensuite which looked new, bathroom and wardrobes for storage. Mary turned to Janice and said, "What do you think, can you see the family living in Rose Cottage?"

Janice thought for a while looking around and then replied, "I think we can make it a very nice place for us and the boys."

Mary smiled, "You can paint it or wallpaper, do what you want, whatever colour within reason, especially the boy's room."

They left to walk down the stairs and Mary told her how they had modernised the cottage after many people had lived in it over the years. Mary took her out the back door into the garden at the rear. It was a fenced, grassed area with plenty of space for the children to run about in and room for their climbing frame and swing. A second section of the garden was an area they could develop into a vegetable patch. It was dug over and had some fruit bushes already in with cages over them to stop the birds eating the fruit. It would be great for the boys to learn how to plant and grow all sorts. It was turning out better than she could have imagined.

On the walk back to the house Janice said she would like to show Harry but Mary informed her that he had already looked round Rose Cottage but was concerned how she would find it before he accepted the job. Janice knew in her heart as she smiled to herself that he knew all along she would be happy with it, and that's why he was certain about accepting the job.

They arrived back at the house via the kitchen, the way they left. Mary offered to do some more tea for everyone but Janice declined as she glanced at her watch. She had not realised how late it was and the boys needed calming down with a bath before bed. They continued to walk back into the lounge and towards the French doors where they had left them all. The boys looked up and saw their mum had returned and rushed excited towards her through the doors. They were telling her all about the tractors they had ridden and she thought it would take a long time to calm them down tonight. She looked up and said to Harry that they really should be going as it was passed the boys' bedtime. Mary and William reassured the boys that their tractors would still be here when they moved in and that they could still play on them. They said their farewells and left for home with two highly excited boys non stop chatting in the back of the car.

When they arrived home Janice took the boys upstairs, with Harry following, he ran them a bath while she got them undressed. They had great fun in the bath with their toys, having exhausted themselves playing outside on the tractors as well, they were ready for bed. Janice managed two pages of the book she was reading to them when they fell asleep. She kissed them good night, turned the light off and pulled the door to as they had a night light in the room to give them comfort. She went downstairs feeling exhausted. It had been an exciting day for her and a lot to look forward to in the future.

Chapter 3

The next morning, there was the question of when was Harry going to start his new job and when could she access the cottage to do some painting. They would have to do something to the boys' room and possibly the lounge.

Over breakfast, which they all sat down to, Harry was able to tell them how things would happen. He would start work in two weeks' time and she could start work on the cottage to have it ready for them while the boys were at nursery school for two days a week. When she was finished they could move in. They would rent the house they lived in now so they always had a house to come back to if it didn't work out. She agreed with the plan. She would start by buying paint as she had some idea for the boys' room. With the boys at nursery that would give her time to get organised. She would contact Mary and arrange when she could start painting and also organising a key from her. She would also be able to have a proper look round the cottage on her own.

She organised the boys with toys and games after breakfast while she started making lists of things to do. It was going to be an adventure for all of them and hopefully a start of something good. She could maybe think about going back to work when the boys were old enough to go full time to school.

Janice rang Mary who said it was not a problem for her to come over in the next week but Mary was disappointed that she would not be bringing the boys with her. Janice thought to her-self they would probably get fed up with them once they had moved in, she will see. Mary was looking forward to have young children around as they had no children or relatives living.

The following week Janice took the boys to nursery and then headed to the cottage, calling into the house for the keys first. She went to the kitchen door, which was open, and the smell of fresh baked bread wafted through the door as she got closer. She heard someone humming. She called out as she knocked and pushed open the door to enter the kitchen. A lady, not Mary, appeared in a pinafore with flour on it, rolling out pastry and humming. Janice cleared her throat and the lady looked up and said, "Hello, can I help you?" Janice explained who she was and the lady said she would go and fetch Mary for her. She washed her hands and then popped off into the hallway calling for Mary. She came back and said Mary would not be long and introduced herself as Margaret, the housekeeper for the house. Janice commented on the bread cooling on the rack and then Margaret offered her a cup of tea with a piece of bread, warm, with butter and jam. She resisted and thanked her but declined the kind offer. Mary walked into the kitchen carrying a plant which looked a bit sorry for itself and in her other hand a lot of dead leaves which she proceeded to put in the bin in the kitchen.

Mary looked up and said to Janice, "Sorry to keep you but had to sort my plants out, they do get neglected sometimes." She went over to where the keys were kept and found Rose Cottage keys and handed them to Janice. She thanked her and took the keys and went to leave as Mary touched her arm and said, "If you need any help at all Margaret and I are willing to help." Janice thanked them both but said she was fine but would keep that in mind but she loved painting in the house and so it was not a problem. She had all her equipment in her car, sheets to cover the carpets and steps as well. She walked out of the house into bright sunlight and walked down the path to the cottage. She had parked the car outside the garage of the cottage in the driveway which was separate from the cottage.

She put the key in the door and turned it with a little hesitation and pushed the door open. Sunlight was coming through the kitchen windows into the hall, casting shadows with strange shapes. A shudder ran down her spine. This was not like her but something had upset her or was she thinking it was haunted as the cottage had a long past. She said to herself, stop being silly, and went back to the car to bring the paint, brushes and everything else she had brought with her. She was going to enjoy herself painting and making the boys' room look lovely. They were at nursery all day for two days a week so she needed to get a move on.

She decided to start in the boys' room first. She went upstairs and went to the room which would be the boys'. She set things up, covering the carpet with her dustsheets. She was going to put colours on different walls and then transfers on one of them. She loved music and put some on to keep her going. The boys loved when she sang songs whether they were popular or nursery songs. She started painting, it went on well. Considering the age of the cottage the walls were not bad at all. She continued, in a world of her own, until she heard someone call her name. She glanced at her watch, lunchtime already. The voice was female and she called down she would be right there in a minute.

She descended the stairs to find Margaret standing

at the bottom carrying a tray with a cloth over it. It was a nice surprise as Janice followed Margaret into the kitchen where she put the tray down for her and lifted the cloth.

Margaret said, "You have home cooked ham, and bread and butter plus some mustard if you like in this pot, and a slice of cake and a jug of lemonade with a glass.

Janice was lost for words, "This is most kind of you, thanks."

She felt hungry now looking at the food and Margaret said goodbye and left her to it. Janice unfolded her deckchair she had brought with her, made the sandwich up with a smear of mustard, poured a glass of lemonade and sat down to eat. The first mouthful was delicious, the cake as well, which she tucked into when she had finished her sandwich. The lemonade was refreshingly good as well. She sat looking into the back garden, planning things in her mind what to do. Vegetable patch for the boys and some fruit trees planted perhaps. Maybe she would draw a plan to show Harry to look at it and he could guide her if he had time with the new job.

Harry would be working with the Head Gardener and another colleague to enable them to keep the grounds and garden looking good all year round, as Mr & Mrs Giles wanted to eventually open it up to the public once it was restored, to raise monies for local charities.

She had swallowed the last mouthful of the cake and was just about to drink the remainder of the lemonade when something caught her eye. Her eye was drawn to a small alcove to one side of the kitchen. She stood up and walked over to the wall to have a close look at a different level, moved her head to locate it in the wall.

She located it and it was wide enough for her to slip her hand inside. She gently moved her hand inside the wall, when her fingers touched something. What was it? A book? No, too small, some papers folded together. She gently tugged at them as she did not want to damage them, not knowing how long they had been there. She continued to gently encourage the papers to come along the gap until a lot of dust and papers emerged. They must have been there a long time. They were yellow with age and covered in dust. Written in faded ink were the words 'poison potions'. Now she gently laid the yellowing papers on the worktop and carefully opened the pages. They were hand written and the words were clearer inside the folded paper. What should she do? She decided to carefully wrap them back up and put them back. She had more pressing work to carry out but she could come back to the alcove in the future and explore more. She would also need to do some research on the Estate and cottage to find out who lived here in the past well before the Giles lived here. Maybe they would be able to help as well.

She carefully put them back in the alcove and went back upstairs to finish the painting of the boys' room before she went to pick them up from nursery. Maybe an exciting discovery lay ahead of her. She would have to be patient.

Chapter 4

The next few weeks followed a pattern. When the boys were at nursery she went to the cottage to paint. Her keys were hers now so she did not have to call at the house any more but a lunchtime tray always appeared. It was all home cooked meat with local cheese, home- made chutney along with something sweet, either a scone or slice of cake and the lemonade so refreshing to wash it all down. She managed to finish the rooms upstairs after a few weeks and the boys' room finished with stencils which looked great. She was proud of the result. She had not touched the old papers in the kitchen since finding them as she needed time to explore them, and at the moment time she did not have to spare.

They had put their house with an agent to rent out so always had a house to return to if the job did not work out. It did not take long to find a tenant and she needed to finish the lounge walls in the Cottage so they could move out. Everything else was ready. Once she finished the walls, they agreed a moving date and got a removal company round, who gave them boxes to pack which the boys loved to play inside. The removal firm agreed to pack the breakables and Janice spoke to Mary to see if the boys could stay with her while the moving went ahead. Mary was over the moon to have them and told her not to worry when the time came.

Janice had started taking small boxes over and unpacking them as well as some clothes, as all the bedrooms had fitted wardrobes like the house she was leaving which made things easy. She was itching to explore the discovered papers in the kitchen but wanted to get moved in and the boys settled. She would be patient.

The moving day came. The feeling of uncertainty and apprehension came over her but the boys were so excited and it would be good for them to have space, safe space to run around. She could not wait to see their faces when they saw the room she had done for them.

She bundled the boys into the car and drove to the Manor house where she was met by Margaret the housekeeper and Mary. They were taken into the room they called the Den to have cookies and milk and sat them down to watch a Thomas the Tank Engine DVD.

Mary said, "That should keep them occupied for a while but we have other things planned to keep them amused so don't worry about them."

"Thanks for your help," Janice said and left to go to Rose Cottage where she would wait for Harry to come with the removal men. She opened the door and wandered from room to room planning where the furniture would go.

The lorry turned up and the removal men said Harry would be along soon as he wanted to clean up the other house before he left. She walked through the house with the guys and said the labels on the doors co-ordinated with the labels on the boxes. She was very organised! They started unloading the lorry and with Janice at the door directing them when they brought in the furniture, to go in certain rooms. They had been unpacking the lorry for an hour when she decided to make a cup of tea. They came into the kitchen to collect it and they all commented on how lovely the Cottage was and its setting. She explained her husband was one of the resident gardeners and that was the reason for the move. They thanked her for the tea and took it outside, just as Harry drove up the drive. He walked up the drive and into the Cottage and she handed him a cup of tea which he gratefully took. He deserved it for cleaning the house they had left. They both propped themselves up against the sink and looked out the window into the garden beyond.

She said, "Do you mind if I change the garden a little to be more child friendly, to have room for swings, a vegetable patch for them to learn how to grow things."

He smiled, "I think that is a great idea and I will help when I have my days off."

"Great" she said and threw her arms around him and kissed him on the cheek.

The removal men returned their mugs to the kitchen and continued to empty the van. Once it was totally unpacked they both thanked them and shut the door. Now for the daunting task of unpacking everything, but first they needed to do the boys' room, beds made and toys unpacked. They would then go and collect them from Mary. They both set to and it was soon done. When it was done Harry said he would collect the boys while Janice continued to unpack and make their bed as well, as they would want an early night no doubt. She had made their bed and was just unpacking some clothes when she heard them.

She entered the landing to be greeted by the boys hurling themselves up the stairs very excited and into her arms. She calmed them down after a few minutes and then took hold of their hands and walked them towards their room. She opened the door and the look and sounds from them made her feel so proud to be a mum to these boys. They loved the new bedding and the stencils on the walls, a new box of toys as well. They asked if they could play with them straight away and she said yes they could. At least they would be occupied and she could get on with the unpacking.

Harry told her that the boys had been given lunch at the House so they did not have to feed them. She needed to start on the kitchen unpacking soon, when Harry called to say a cup of tea he had done was waiting for her, so she popped her head into the boys' room to let them know she would be downstairs if they wanted her. She needed a break and she felt tired.

When she walked into the kitchen/diner the table was laid with a lovely salad for her. She looked at him. He shrugged his shoulders and said it was here when he walked in. They pulled up the chairs, and started eating. Neither of them realised how hungry they were. While eating Harry put his knife and fork down and said,

"They have asked us to dinner tonight, including the boys. I hope you don't mind but I said yes?"

She smiled, "Of course not, I will be able to unpack more boxes without wondering what to do for tea."

She continued eating, thinking that actually this has worked well and was a good opportunity to get some background information about the history of the Manor and the previous occupants of Rose Cottage. When she finished her lunch she started on unpacking boxes for the kitchen and was helped by Harry who periodically checked on the boys in their bedroom, who were still playing.

The time had come to go over to the Manor for dinner so Janice gathered up the children with Harry and went over. They entered via the kitchen as instructed. Upon opening the door, pushing it slowly open, the wonderful smell that met them made their mouths water. It was roast beef with all the trimmings plus lots of vegetables from the garden. The boys tugged at her hands, which were being held as they walked through the kitchen as Margaret left off from what she was doing and greeted them and showed them through to the lounge, where Mr and Mrs Giles were waiting with drinks for them all. There was a selection for the boys to choose from which Mrs Giles had organised, and Mr Giles had sorted the grown-ups their drinks.

Mary put the boys' drinks on a low table for them with some crisps to keep them happy before dinner, which would not spoil their appetite. Janice had a gin and tonic and so did Harry. They both settled on the settee and William and Mary joined them and asked how the move had gone and were they settled in. Janice thought of asking about past occupants of both the Manor and Rose Cottage but Margaret popped her head round the corner of the door and asked Mary to join her for a moment. The boys looking up as she left the room and then looked at Janice in anticipation she knew, for food. She patted the settee for them to join her and she asked if they needed to go to the toilet before they sat down at the table for dinner. They both nodded and Janice excused herself and asked to be pointed in the direction of the toilet to take the boys. After a short while she came back just in time to be called to the dining room with William leading the way.

They sat down at the table with a wonderful spread before them. Roast beef, Yorkshire pudding, roast and mashed potatoes, peas, carrots and courgettes from the garden and homemade horseradish sauce. The boys' eyes were as large as saucers. Mary had provided booster seats for the boys' courtesy of Margaret's daughters and she sat them both between Harry and herself so they could both deal with them. They took it in turns putting the food on the boys' plates and then their own. They cut the food up for the boys to eat and told them it was okay to start. They all enjoyed the home cooked meal, it was lovely to taste fresh produce from the garden, which was so much better than shop bought.

During the meal Janice started to make conversation about how long the Giles' had been in the house and also the occupancy of Rose Cottage. Harry turned several times to look at her, meaning stop interrogating them, but she needed to know the history. The Giles had not been in the Manor house long, ten years in fact, but they bought it for a bargain price as it was a little run down and they wanted to bring it back to its former glory especially the garden. Therefore they did some looking into the history themselves and William offered to give her some books he had found about the history of the Estate including Rose Cottage. She thanked him and said she would collect the books in a few days-time, once they had settled in properly and were fully unpacked.

There was a choice of puddings, homemade trifle and apple pie and custard. The boys' went for trifle along with Janice, and Harry went for the apple pie. After the delicious meal they went into the lounge and had a cup of tea and coffee. The boys were getting tired and cuddled their mum on the settee so she skipped the tea, thanked the host and headed back to the Cottage with two very sleepy boys. They passed through the kitchen where Margret passed them a parcel of food to help them tomorrow to feed everyone. Janice thanked her for her kindness and went out of the kitchen door with the boys and Harry to their new home Rose Cottage.

It was a short walk. They had forgotten to put a light on outside the Cottage but Harry had a torch which helped. Harry took the boys upstairs to get them ready for bed and Janice took the food to the kitchen and put it away. The appliances had been delivered a few days before so were up and running. She joined Harry upstairs to help put the boys to bed and he left her reading them a story. It wasn't long before they were sound asleep. There was a night light on the landing for them which would help them if they woke in the night.

She went downstairs to find Harry in the lounge with a night-cap in his hand and one waiting for her. She plonked herself down on the settee and let out a long sigh.

Harry said, "You look exhausted, but we had a good meal at the Manor and I think we will all enjoy living here don't you?"

Janice agreed wholeheartedly and lent over to give him a kiss on the cheek. They would shortly follow the boys to bed after their night cap, as it had been a long day for them and still plenty of things to look forward to.

Chapter 5

The next few days Harry was around to help either unpack boxes, amuse the boys or just help to put up curtains, blinds and pictures. The boys were due to start the new nursery at the local school now. Being a village, they took them at an earlier age of 4. Janice thought it would give her the freedom of going to get the books from the Manor as promised and start her research into the history of the families that had lived here. If she had names, births and deaths she could go and search on the computer for a few hours.

Janice arrived at the village school and was among a few other mums with their children, so she introduced herself and the boys. She went inside with the others, and the boys were off before she knew it to play with the toys. She was reassured that they would settle in quickly and only had to fill in some forms with the clerk and then left. She was reassured as she left that they would have no problem settling in.

On her way back she drove to the front entrance of the Manor, and used the front door this time, as she did not like using the entrance via the kitchen. She rang the door-bell and William answered. Upon opening the door and seeing it was Janice he invited her in while apologising for Mary not being in as she had gone to town for a few things. Janice explained she was here for the books that they had discussed the other night at dinner. He invited her into the Study where they were and opened the door. She followed him into the room and found herself inside an oak panelled room with bookshelves fitted against most of the walls with numerous books, some looking extremely old. It did not take him long to find what he was looking for. There were three books. One was slightly dog-eared, old, and was The History of Falcon Manor. That was its original name and William said that it was very helpful to him when he was doing research. He explained that the book had a lot of historical facts plus pictures of the people who lived in the Manor House.

He gave her another book he thought would be helpful along with some old records relating to who worked in the Manor house as well as recording accounts and wages. There was also another one which he thought she would find useful as well. She thanked him as he showed her out and wished her good luck in her research. He added that if he could help in any way for her to just ask him.

She walked back to Rose Cottage clutching her books, imagining what they would reveal. She had a little time before she picked the boys up so she thought she would look at them. She made herself a cup of tea and sat down at the table with the books in front of her. Where would she start first? She took one and opened it, then glanced out at the garden, mug in her hands, when out of the corner of her eye she noticed something. Of course it was the alcove where the papers she found were.

She stood up and walked over to the alcove and pushing in her fingers to locate the papers, slowly pulling them out. She bought them over to the table, pushing the books to one side while she carefully unfolded the yellowing papers. She started to look at the words on the yellowing paper and looked more closely and saw what she thought was a drawing of a plant or flower of some sort. She studied the writing which was written in very curvy letters. She stood up and went over to where a pen and pad was, and brought it to the table so she could write the words down as she deciphered it. She found it difficult as some of the writing was so faint. The first couple of words she thought said 'I want to stop this madness.'

She would start with that and try to see what she could read and leave blanks or just put a letter if she could not decide what it was supposed to be. It took some time to string a couple of sentences together, and then she glanced up at the clock. Time had run away with her again. She carefully folded the old paper up and put it back in the alcove to hide it. She was not ready to share with anyone at this time. The words she had written on a piece of paper went inside one of the books which she then went to put in the study, safely away. She grabbed her keys and coat and was off out of the door to pick the boys up from school.

She repeated the same things for the next couple of days until she had written down as much as she could with a few word guesses here and there. Then one day she sat back and looked at what she had so far and read it out loud.

'I want to stop this madness now, it hurts and I know I cannot complain. It is my job but (unreadable word) madness is gaining strength. What do I do the (unreadable word) is strong.'

Then there was this picture of a plant? The other paper looked like a recipe but maybe just a list of things? She was not sure what. First she needed to look through some plant books that her husband had and she might recognise it. This would take sometime but she could not show Harry the picture just yet, only as a last resort.

What was this person going through and how long ago did it take place? She needed to look at the

96

history of the occupancy of the house, and see the records of the servants that had worked and lived in Rose Cottage.

She would work on the history of the occupancy of The Manor House and Rose Cottage and try and piece together who may have written the note. She had a lot to do so she had to be patient in her hunt. When she found time she started to look through the books William lent her, and she would make notes, then go to the other books to cross reference if she could to clarify things. She started collecting together the previous owners and names of the servants and gardening staff. Some of it was easy as the books for the estate showed names and amounts they were paid, and the years they were employed, and who occupied Rose Cottage.

From the lists she made it was interesting as the occupancy of Rose Cottage was not continuous. This might become a problem for her trying to find the person who left the note. She needed to go to the local library for help to see if they had records of births and deaths, as the Manor was owned by the Bryant family for hundreds of years until the line died out. It was left in disrepair until the Giles family bought it. She needed also to decide when to start discussing it with her husband. It would depend on when she found out who left the note, and if it indicated an event happening in the Manor or Rose Cottage. She had to be patient as this would all take time.

She settled into a routine whereby she would take the boys to school and then visit the library, where she joined a class who were looking into ancestors. This class was for an hour and she had access to computers for research on different websites. She started looking at the census in the 1911. She discovered a census has been taken every ten years since 1801 with the exception of 1941. The 1841 census was the first to list names of every individual.

The records from the Manor were dated both before and after 1911 and there were female servants' names. She thought that would be a start. Working her way through it, she came across a girl called Alice Hart who had worked as a maid in the Manor which she found in the census and was single.

When she checked the Manor records a few years later her name was not there. Therefore she decided to look at deaths to see if she could find anything. The records showed she had died from some sort of poison. She put together what she had found in the papers at the Cottage, along with the information she had uncovered plus the records from the Manor, and concluded that maybe she was pregnant by someone in the household, which used to happen.

Janice also discovered that the plant drawing was actually Yew, grown on the estate. She also found a very interesting book in the library about poisonous plants/shrubs/trees. Within this book it stated that Yew berries were used in Victoria days to abort pregnant women but when the poison was taken very often they were accidently overdosed and died. Survival was rare.

The papers and the words looked to point to the maid falling in love with someone at the Manor in the 1900's and writing the note. Finding herself pregnant, she took the drastic steps of abortion with the terrible consequence of her dying. It was such a pity, for someone to die at such a young age.

After a month of discovering the details she shared it with her husband, Harry. He was fascinated at what she had discovered and the use of the Yew as a poison. She showed him the yellowed papers she found and they wondered whether to share the details with the Giles family but for the time being they decided not to show them. That might seem strange but time will tell why.

Chapter 6

Many years passed, the children grew up in the wonderful environment of the estate grounds and were also welcomed in the Manor House by Mary and William. But as they grew, over the years they spent more and more time with them rather than with Janice. She became resentful and envious of the close relationship that built between her boys and Mary and William. It was the little things at first. Tea after school, special meals of their favourite foods, gifts that they could not afford to buy. Harry dismissed the way she felt and told her not to be so silly and jealous as the boys loved being spoilt. He was now Head Gardner of the Estate and did not want to upset anything that would affect his job.

As time went by the resentment became hatred, which grew to such an extent she wanted to get rid of Mary and William. She had to put a plan in place without her husband knowing what she had in mind, otherwise he would stop her. She would have to plan ways to persuade Mary and William to change their will to give the children the house and estate when they died, to be kept in Trust until they were old enough, say 30, but giving her and Harry legal rights to run the Estate until then. She plotted in her mind that it needed to be worked on sooner rather than later, as the boys would soon be off to University, and also their health was a consideration, she did not want an early death and plans had not been put in place.

She started plotting her deceitful plan in her mind as she had an excellent memory for things like this. She hated them so much because the boys were so fond of them both and spent so much time with them.

She had to do something that would benefit her.

Her first step was involving herself with the boys at the Manor house and not being so aloof with Mary and William. This was hard for her but she made an effort over the coming months, then she felt she could progress to talking about the will and the boys.

She was caught off guard when one evening when the boys were having a sleep over at the Manor, when they were invited for a drink, as they wanted to discuss an important matter with her and Harry. They both went over that night and as they arrived William offered them a drink and they all sat down together.

William started the conversation, "You know we have no relatives we would like to leave the Manor House and Estate to."

"Yes," Harry said.

William went on to say "Well Mary and I have decided we would like your boys to inherit the Manor House and Estate when we die."

Janice looked at Harry, showing signs she hoped of shock.

"We are both overwhelmed by your generosity but would ask if it could be in Trust until they reach the age of 30 as we do not know how the boys will be after they have been to University. It might change their outlook on things," said Janice.

William laughed, "Yes you have a point, I can remember when I was a young adult. So we would be happy to leave you and Harry as Executors of the Estate until the boys became 30."

Janice said, "That would be a good idea then we can guide them in the running of the Estate and lead them into the job slowly."

William replied nodding, "Great plan. I will make an appointment with the Solicitors as soon as possible and let you know when it is so that you can both come to see them at the same time."

They all picked up their drinks and toasted to the future of the Estate, knowing it would be left in good hands.

Janice could not have wished for a better result without her having to push them into the decision. But she still wanted that Manor house all to herself and she would find a way to do it. In the back of her mind a thought about the yellow paper and the poison made from Yew berries was there. Not too soon, as that would look suspicious.

A few days later and they were all off to the Solicitors. They went in separate cars and arrived at the office not long after each other. They waited until they were ushered into the office, Mary and William sitting in front of the Solicitor's desk and Janice and Harry a little back from the desk on the side of the room.

The Solicitor addressed William and Mary first. "I understand that you want me to change your will to allow the Estate to go to the children you are not related to when you both die, is that correct?"

William replied, "Yes we would like to put it in Trust for the boys until they get to the age of 30. If there is time before that, we wish to have their parents as Executors and to run the Estate until such time they reach the age of 30."

The Solicitor said, "I will draw something up for you to look at but you may want to think about if the boys do not live to that age, you should look at all things that may happen."

William went on to say he wanted both Harry and Janice to oversee the Estate before the boys came of age to take over. He also said in case one of the boys or both were not interested in running the Estate for it to be sold, and each boy given half the estate but for Rose Cottage to be left to Harry and Janice for the rest of their lives.

The Solicitor said he would draw up a draft to allow everything they had asked for to be put in and arranged for William and Mary to come back and see him at a later date.

Janice turned to William and said, "Are you sure you wish to do this?"

"Yes" said William. "They have been like our own sons and we want to give them something back for all the years of pleasure they have given us." Janice rose and went over to William who also stood up and they embraced.

They all stood now as William thanked the Solicitor and left the room together. They met up later, as arranged at the Manor House, with the boys present, to involve them in what had been agreed. Janice and Harry were hoping for the boys to be encouraged to go to college or university to study horticulture or business studies to help them run the Estate in the future before they were 30. She was hoping once the boys had left home she would start thinking on how she could put her plan in place but not too soon after the boys left. She would have to wait a little time to put her plan in place.

They met up in the lounge with drinks and nibbles waiting for them all. The boys had arrived back from school and changed before going to the Manor, and as they all walked into the lounge, given a drink and sat down. It was William who wanted to tell the boys what he was planning to do, and as he cleared his voice he turned to them and said, "Mary and I have decided to give you boys a chance to inherit the

Estate as and when you reach the age of 30. By that time you will have made your way in life and know what you want."

He then turned towards their parents and said, "It will be kept in trust until as and when both of us die with your parents being the trustees of the Estate."

The boys both turned to their parents and said, "What if we do not want to keep the Estate?"

Janice replied, "It is a long time away, we shall decide what to do as and when the time arrives."

That seemed to settle the boys as William poured drinks, the boys getting juice. They toasted the future and hopefully the future of the Estate being passed on to someone who would cherish it and not sell it off for building land in the future.

In the next year Janice had a plan that with the boys off her hands, she would become more involved in the running of the Manor House to help the housekeeper, Margaret, as she was getting to the stage of not being able to carry out the chores around the house. Mary was getting older as well and could not help as much as she used to.

The plan Janice had was that she would help more and more with the housework first, then help with the cooking when Margaret stepped down from the job. Then she would have access to what Mary and William ate. Her plan was coming together but she needed to be patient.

Chapter 7

A few years had passed and the boys were both away at University now. They both decided to do business studies neither of them was interested in the horticultural side which disappointed Harry a great deal. He was hoping one of them at least would have shown some interest in the work on the Estate especially now he had re-established all the old gardens. This included the walled garden that grew all the vegetables and fruit for the Estate. With more help from the boys he thought he could concentrate on a few more projects he had in mind to carry out.

Harry was so green fingered he could make anything grow, even when all the other gardeners had given up on the plants. He breathed life into them. He had the touch and care no one else had. He had won many awards for the Estate. William was so happy with what had been won, even though he was unable to help in the garden because of his mobility problems as he got older. He encouraged Harry to enter the flower and vegetable shows in the village as well as the County shows. He was becoming well known for his green fingers!

William one day was pottering in the greenhouse where Harry was encouraging the plants to grow by playing music. Yes, Harry believed in it and thought it helped the plants grow. Harry walked into the greenhouse and looked at him and said, "You okay William? You look a bit tired."

William replied, "No I am okay but wish I was like your plants, energised by the music. I am not getting any younger and neither is Mary."

Harry laughed, "You do alright for your age."

They both laughed and agreed. Harry brought his flask out which he always had, and the two of them sat down with a couple of mugs and poured the tea from the flask and put the world to right. They enjoyed each other's company.

Janice on the other hand was now working in the Manor house, the kitchen especially. She had made a cake for Mary, and was preparing a pot of tea for her, and cut a slice of cake which no doubt William would share with her later. Janice thought about how she would kill them but she would only kill one at a time. She would use the yew berries crushed and put in a strong tasting stew perhaps?

It would be like in the Victorian days where they gave pregnant ladies the yew mixture to abort but tended to overdose and kill them. But would the poison be traced in the body afterwards? She was not sure. She would take a gamble and make plans to go ahead with poisoning Mary first. What she did not know was things would change suddenly and be out of her control.

She decided she would use six of the berries crushed up in Mary's food, a stew of meat and herbs and turmeric. She had read that the berries were potent and quickly absorbed. She would hope William would not want to taste it so she would do it when he was not about, say going into town to see his golfing friends for lunch or with Harry at an event. She would have to wait for the right moment. The plan in place in her mind, she got on with her work and took the tray into Mary with the tea and cake.

She did not have to wait long, as she found out William was going with Harry for an event in two weeks' time so she would put her plan in place for then.

That morning came when William and Harry went off to the event. The only problem was William wanted to eat with Mary when he got back so Janice had to plan for two stews, one each, the poison going into Mary's stew only. Janice said her farewells to them both and started preparing the meals to cook later.

Janice had already collected the berries from the tree itself rather that the nursery area so she would not be seen. As she was preparing all the vegetables, Mary walked into the kitchen looking very pale and turned to Janice and said, "I do not feel well at all, I have pains in my arm and chest." When Janice looked up from the sink where she was preparing the vegetables, Mary collapsed on the floor. Janice panicked; she did not know what to do. She was taken aback. She bent down to check Mary, and rang for the ambulance. They came into the kitchen and gave her oxygen. Once stable they transferred her to the ambulance and Janice followed in her car. While driving, she rang Harry from her hands free phone and told him what had happened. He said they would meet her at the hospital as soon as they could. It was serious and she was not sure how long she would hang on to life.

She arrived at the hospital and was taken into an area to wait while Mary was taken into a cubicle. She waited a while until they came and got her, to say they were sorry but they could not save her, she had had a massive heartattack.

William and Harry arrived too late but William was taken in to see her while Harry comforted Janice. It was while he was comforting her she realised fate had had a hand in what she had planned. She did not

107

have to poison her at all, so she could use it on William instead. She snapped out of it and spoke to Harry to tell him what happened. They were offered tea and a lot later William joined them. He was red eyed and wet cheeked.

William was in shock when they got home. They rang the GP and he came out and gave something to help William, and Harry put him to bed. They both decided to stay the night to keep an eye on him. They had been told at the hospital that the death certificate would be available quickly as they knew what the cause of death was, and as she had been seeing the doctor about high blood pressure it would not be a problem.

Janice needed also to get rid of the poison she had prepared to add to the stew as soon as possible without Harry seeing her and questioning her, or him accidently using the mixture. Panic now set in, as they made their way downstairs after settling William into bed and making the spare bed up for themselves.

Janice said, "You go into the lounge and make yourself comfy while I go and make a sandwich and coffee in the kitchen and bring it in." Harry nodded, he looked exhausted. She hurried into the kitchen, saw where she had left the poison in a pot and went to pick it up not knowing what to do with it. She hesitated. It could go into the bin she thought but someone might find it. She needed to dispose of it another way away from the house. What could she do? She was not thinking straight after what had happened. She tried flushing it down the sink, but it did not work as she was left with a thick lump of berries. She quickly got some newspaper and wrapped it all up and put it outside the kitchen door to deal with it later. She would make an excuse later to go to Rose Cottage and put it on the compost heap. That way it would not be connected to her she hoped.

She washed her hands, made the sandwiches and boiled the kettle and made the tea, and took them both into the lounge on a tray where Harry was. She sat down and poured him a hot mug of tea and added a spoonful of sugar - which he did not normally take - as well as a sandwich. He looked exhausted. He said, "We need to make sure William is okay, he has taken it hard."

She nodded and replied, "Yes I will make sure he eats well and we need to help him deal with the funeral as he can't do it himself."

Harry agreed and also said when they had more details to tell the boys as they would want to be at the funeral.

Janice made an excuse and left him, while she went and carried out what she had planned with the poisonous berries. She was deep in thought while she picked up the package she left outside the kitchen door. She walked over to Rose Cottage. She stopped and thought – what happens if the boys come home and upset her plan to take over the Estate? She walked on. She made her way round to the back of the cottage and through the gate and towards the compost heap. She placed some vegetable peelings on top of the poison.

She made her way back to the house as a wave of nausea came over her. She had to calm herself by slow breathing. She had to somehow talk the boys out of any ideas they had of giving up on their education.

She walked through the kitchen door and into the main house, and Harry was standing there in the hall. She was caught off guard. "Where have you been?"

He asked.

"Just had to go to Rose Cottage to check on things as we will be sleeping here tonight won't we?" pushing it back to him.

She saw him relax his body and he said, "I will go and check on William I think."

He came back into the lounge to say William was still asleep probably due to what the GP had given him. She suggested to Harry to go to bed and she would lock up the house and join, him but before she did that she needed to eat her sandwich which she had not eaten.

The next few days were sorting the funeral arrangements, Janice helping him along the way to help him get through it, while Harry continued running the Estate as usual.

She was heartless with William, putting thoughts in his head about how would he cope without his wife now, and life would not be worth living, and how could he live in the house with so much reminding him of her. She was planting seeds and hoped he would die of a broken heart perhaps rather than have to poison him.

She was cold and calculating. How had she got to be like this? Envy is an evil which takes you over if you let it. Her need to have the Estate and house to herself was overwhelming her now. She wanted to be Lady of the Estate and to have her own servants running after her, and why not?

Chapter 8

The day of the funeral was a struggle for William. He had tranquillizers from the doctor to help him. This made him a little out of it but he was supported by Harry. The boys were there as well, as Janice had told them about what had happened and to only come to the funeral as their parents would handle everything else in connection with the Estate. They reluctantly accepted the situation and after the funeral went back to university.

After the funeral William was not very well. He would walk around the house lost in his thoughts. Harry went back to work on the Estate, checking in on him in the evening. Janice would prepare dinner which they all ate in the kitchen before Janice and Harry headed back to Rose Cottage to sleep. This continued for a few months but William was not good. He seemed depressed.

One day Janice sat down with William in the kitchen and over a cup of tea they talked about how things would be better if the will was changed again to allow her and Harry to run the Estate and get rid of the Trust that was set up. She went on to convince him they would look after the Estate better than the boys would and they would pass it to them when they died. In fact she said they could all change their wills at the same time to re-assure him. He said he would think about it for a week or two and discuss it again. She looked after the house and cooked for him and made sure he ate. It was a struggle and she kept reminding him of the discussion they had.

Then one morning when she came in to the kitchen to make lunch for him, he was sitting at the table already. She was surprised. William looked up and said, "I have decided to change the will and have made an appointment for us all to go down to the Solicitors, I hope that is okay with you both."

Janice said, "Yes that is fine we will make it okay. You won't regret it. Harry will do so much to restore things for you on the Estate."

William stood up and hugged her. She thought to herself, great she can proceed to the next plan soon. She was so cold and calculating.

They went ahead to the Solicitor with William. He altered his will and Harry and Janice theirs. William seemed to rally after it was done, so much so she was only cooking meals in the evening for him. But she was finding empty bottles of wine, more than usual, and felt she needed to speak to him about it. He was taking antidepressants as well, and maybe this would enable her to get rid of him rather than use the poison she was thinking of. Maybe she could get him to overdose by accident?

This particular evening when she walked into the kitchen to see him, he was sitting at the kitchen table. A bottle of whisky was by his hand on the table, half empty. She cleared her throat. He looked up, his eyes red from crying. Now she thought would be a good time to work on him.

Janice said, "The answer is not in a bottle you know. If you continue like this you will forget when you have taken your tablets and maybe accidently overdose on them."

William looked at her, "You know I see her around the house, calling to me, it is so hard for me."

Janice wondered if he had heard what she had just said but it did not matter, as she felt he was not far away from committing suicide he was in such a state. She could help things along with crushed tablets in warm milk much better than the crushed yew berries.

She made some tea and left it for him on the table to eat. He thanked her and she left him pushing the food around his plate. She went in the next evening and was not surprised to see dirty dishes left everywhere. He was giving up on life she thought. She went to look for him, calling his name. No reply. She looked in the lounge and study. She decided to go upstairs to see if he had gone to bed to sleep the alcohol off. She looked up the stairs and slowly mounted every step towards the landing, each making eerie noises of creaking until she was standing on the landing. She looked across to William's door which was closed. She gingerly got hold of the handle of the door, turned it to unlatch the door, and pushed it open.

He was laid across the bed full dressed. Her heart jumped. Had he collapsed from drink? She walked forward and gently touched him to see if she could find a pulse, but there was nothing. She gently lowered herself onto the bed and said, "You are with her now and at peace. Thank you, you do not know what you have done for me."

She stood up and ran down the stairs, rushing out of the kitchen door heading for Rose Cottage. She burst through the door making Harry jump. "What's the matter?"

"It's William, he is not breathing. Come quick, I think he has taken his life."

They both ran over to the Manor, from Rose Cottage and while Janice called the ambulance, Harry ran up the stairs two at a time to check the situation. Harry had not come down the stairs so she presumed

William was dead. The ambulance arrived after ten minutes. She let them in and showed them upstairs, calling out for Harry at the same time. He met them on the landing and took them into William's bedroom.

Janice started pacing the floor downstairs wondering what they were doing. Then after a while all came downstairs and confirmed that William was dead. They said that the police had to be informed due to the circumstances of the death. They all went into the lounge and Janice re-assured the ambulance crew she was okay and they then went out of the room with Harry. They would wait for the police. As they were waiting Harry made a cup of tea for Janice to help her with the shock of finding William.

He took the tea to her and said was she okay while he dealt with the police. She nodded. The Police had come into the kitchen and were talking to the ambulance crew who were still there. Harry took the police upstairs to the bedroom while another officer went into the lounge to speak to Janice. He asked her questions and wrote down her replies. After a few minutes Harry returned and joined her where he was questioned as well. They talked for a few minutes more before another officer came from seeing the body upstairs.

He told them, "We found a note among the empty pill bottles and we also found an empty spirit bottle under the bed as well."

"The note indicated he took his own life and no doubt what you have told the officer here of the home situation will hopefully clarify matters."

The officer went on to say that an autopsy would have to be carried out and the family would be notified. Harry said that William had no family except them. The officer nodded and suggested that they stay in the room while they deal with things. He would come and let them know when they had finished and removed the body.

Harry turned to Janice and said, "We don't seem to be blessed in the last few months with the two deaths to deal with." Janice just nodded and drank her tea, trying to look sad, hiding the feeling of joy that she would now inherit what she felt was rightly hers all along.

Things progressed as things do with another funeral to arrange and organise. Then there was the reading of the will which meant Harry and Janice had now been handed what she had always wanted-the Manor House and Estate. She would be lady of the Manor with servants running after her. She had money to make the inside of the house just how she wanted it. Harry had no stomach for all that. He was only interested in the Estate and Gardens.

Janice auctioned most of the contents of the Manor house, only keeping old pictures relating to the history of the house, and she pushed them into the study, which she did not change. She redecorated in her style and used some of her furniture and things from Rose Cottage but bought lots of new and expensive items as well. She put her stamp on the house. They decided to let Rose Cottage rather than give it to one of the gardeners. That way they would get some extra income coming in.

Harry expanded the greenhouse and vegetable growing, as well as the fruit, which he set up to sell all the extras that were grown within their shop on the Estate now.

Many years later, Janice had a need to say something to Harry about what she had planned to do, poison both Mary and William, whereby she would get her hands on the Manor House and be 'Lady of the Manor'. She had been feeling guilty at what she had planned and during one evening when they were both enjoying themselves, relaxing by the roaring fire, with a drink in their hands she turned to him. Not knowing what reaction she would get but prepared for the worst, she said, "Harry I have to tell you something which I am not proud of but hope you will understand why."

THE MAGIC TOUCH

Chapter 1

She opened the cottage door. It creaked. She looked across to the Estate agent guy who was showing her around, and he mouthed sorry to her. Then he said the cottage had not been lived in for some time. The owner had died under suspicious circumstances, and so there was a delay in selling the property, and he went on to say there had been gossip about the circumstances but he did not believe in that sort of thing.

They continued to move around the rooms in the cottage. Sally had always dreamed of having a cottage so she could use it as a retreat or holiday place. It did need a lot of work but she would work her magic as she did on all her projects. This did not seem too bad but to be sure would need a survey on it just to make sure. She loved a project to get her teeth into.

After she had seen enough she asked to go back with the guy from the Estate agent to his office where she would put an offer in subject to the survey. They went to his office where they sat down to negotiate. She would go ahead with the survey but adjust her offer if something bad showed up. He said he could not promise that would be accepted, but no one else had shown any interest at the moment, so he felt it was not a problem.

She thanked him and then, deep in thought, knew it needed a damp proof course just by looking and the age of the cottage. She also needed the roof trusses and all woodwork checking for woodworm infestation and anything else they might find. She hoped that was not the case and the roof was given a clean bill of health, otherwise it would be very costly for her now she had set her heart on it.

She turned to the guy and said, "I will offer say £120,000 subject to the surveyor's report as I may have to adjust the figure, and I will give you my solicitor's details as well. I will organise the surveyor immediately and he will be in touch directly with you."

The guy looked at her. "Well we don't normally work like this, please excuse me while I get in touch with the owner." He went into another room to make a phone call.

That left her thinking of the plan. She had done this type of work many times now, but usually selling them on, but this time she was maybe thinking of keeping this cottage for herself. She would see how it worked out.

The guy returned to her at the desk and said, "The owners have not got a problem as this has been the only interest so far after such a long time on the market. They are willing to see what the survey turns up and will re-negotiate with you on the result of the report."

She stood up and shook his hands, and said that the surveyor should be in touch in the next couple of days. She walked out of the door, took her phone out of her bag and looked for Dan's number. She dialled it, and it was ringing. He answered after the fourth ring. "Hi, Dan I need to ask a favour and hope you are well," she said.

Dan replied, "Nice to hear from you too. Long time since we spoke and I presume you have found another project to do and that is the only reason you phone me." She laughed.

She explained what she needed doing and it was

like most jobs, to be done like yesterday. She gave him the details of the Estate Agents to contact and the address of the property and what she required, which was a full and thorough survey due to the age of the property. She said he could text her when he was going as she was staying in the area and could meet him at the property. Dan said not a problem and he would be in touch. She finished the call and returned to the Estate Agent to let them know it would be Dan contacting them for access. The guy was grateful she was so quick and thanked her.

She left and headed for a coffee shop. She needed to make notes for herself. She was walking along the high street and came across a lovely looking coffee shop and went in and found a table. She sat down and the waitress came and took her order, tea and scone. She set to work on her project.

The kitchen needed ripping out totally, re-plumbing, re-wired, heating replaced unless it was a new boiler, if so that may save her some money. Fireplaces she may keep but the windows need replacing as some were rotten and upvc are longer lasting. The tea and scones were very enjoyable but back to work. She needed to contact her team. She always used Benny and Franky. Yes there name is a bit like that ice cream firm, that's why they reversed it and changed Frankie to Franky.

She found them when she started doing her first house after selling her father's business after his death. It was too much for her to run. She contacted the guys and they thought she was going to be a push over seeing she was a woman but they were really mistaken. She knew her stuff coming from a building background with her father and she took no prisoners. They soon learnt who was boss when working with her and they respected her for it. They would always listen to her ideas and would only cross swords when things were really impossible to do.

She rang Franky. It went to voice mail and so she left a message saying she was starting a new project in about four weeks' time and needed them to be on board with her, so could they get in touch with her. She put the phone down and finished her scone.

She now needed to contact her accountant to make sure the money would be made available for her to make the transaction as and when it happened. Jim was an old friend of her father's who when he had the business was his accountant. Sally sold her father's building business as it was too much for her to continue with but decided to use the money in a different way. This was to buy properties throughout the country in good situations but needing either total refurbishment or just a few jobs doing then either rent or sell them off. She loved getting her hands dirty and she made money as well. She had a magic touch when it came to doing up property.

She paid the bill and left the café then dialled Jim's number. He was with a client so she left a message with his assistant for him to call her as soon as possible. Now she had to be patient to wait and hear back from Dan. This was hard for her as she could not wait to get stuck into this project. She could look into bathroom and kitchen companies and what was available so decided to go back to the hotel room and do some searching on line. The company she usually used for both was a bit far for her to go now so some research would help her choose more quickly. She had done this so many times that she knew what worked and what didn't, but if this was going to be where she would actually live from now on she would choose differently.

She got back to the hotel room and found the computer and started her searches. She went on the kitchen website first. She needed light colours as the windows were small and wanted to make it as light as possible. She would choose cream units and light tiles with a darker work top and a two toned floor tile, but not too light. She looked at the pictures but she did not want something too modern or too old fashioned. She was about half an hour before she found the right one she was looking for. It was a cream shaker style door that she liked and she made a note of the range and code numbers. While she was still looking at the work tops she rang her contact.

He answered. He recognised her voice. She told him the range she wanted and needed to know what the delivery was like and was it possible within her schedule. Yes it fitted in time wise so she gave him details plus the worktop she had found to compliment it. She agreed that once exchange of contacts had happened they would come down and measure up but in the mean time she would email a rough design for him to work on. He said not to bother, that he would pop down next week to meet her and he would measure and go over the design together. She thanked him and put the phone down, recording things in her book as well. Each project had a book that recorded everything.

She closed the computer and lay down on the bed for a second before her phone rang. She answered. It was Franky. They had a long chat about this project and he was fine as he would always drop everything for Sally as she was a valued friend and customer. She went through her plan for the place, barring any surprises the survey might show and said she would give him as much lead in time as possible. She thanked him and put the phone down. She lay down again, feeling slightly exhausted and closed her eyes.

Sally was woken by her phone an hour later. She must have dropped off. It was Jim returning her call. He asked, "How are you, keeping well I hope? I see you have another new project. You never stop to smell the grass."

Sally replied, "What do you mean? Well let's get on with business shall we. So what is the bottom line on my spending on this project?"

Jim then went on to ask more details of the property, the purchaser price she was talking about and the working figure she wanted to spend on the interior as well as anything outside. Then she surprised him and said, "I may even end up living and staying in this one."

Jim laughed, and replied, "Gypsy! No way, can't see it, but I'll go along with your plans and you have £200,000 to £250,000 to play with but try and keep it below if you can."

Sally said, "Okay Jim you keep me in order."

Jim replied back, "Yeah, whenever have I been able to do that."

Sally thanked him. In fact she owed him a lot as after her father died he helped her keep it together in many ways. She put the phone down again and looking across to the clock did not realise it was that late. She jumped into the shower and changed to go down to dinner, as she had just realised she was starving.

She picked up her note book as she left the room to go to dinner. She was shown to a table and sat down looking around the room as she did. A mixed selection of people sat at the tables. She loved to people watch and was good at it with years of practice. She could spot the furtive couple away for a naughty weekend as well as other people she spotted in her many visits to many hotels. The waiter distracted her, asking her if she wanted a drink as she looked at the menu. She asked for a glass of wine and when he brought it over to her table she ordered her meal from the menu.

After he left the table she looked at her project book and started writing in it. Rewiring, replumbing (possibly), new windows, doors, as well as plastering. Then another section of the book possible damp proof course, wood preservation, roof overhaul, guttering and pointing. She had a love hate relationship with older properties and would try and steer clear of them if she could. She had done a few in her time and sometimes they would hide wonderful surprises like discovering hidden inglenook fireplaces. She also knew the pitfalls of dry rot!

She finished her meal and went back up to her room and went onto her laptop to look at bathrooms this time. Looking at the layout she was wondering how she could squeeze another shower in upstairs when her phone bleeped. It was a text message. She looked at it and it was from Dan. He would be here tomorrow and at the cottage for 2pm as he had had a cancellation. She replied to his text, thanking him and said she would see him at the property.

She put her phone down and continued her search of bathrooms, then colour schemes and then looked at furniture. An hour had passed and she had felt she had wasted too much time, closed the computer and got ready for bed. She was looking forward to meeting Dan and hoped he did not find too much wrong with the cottage. Otherwise it would be costing her too much to make any go of it.

Chapter 2

Sally got up in the morning, had breakfast, and amused herself like she could the rest of the morning. She had some lunch in town and then headed to the cottage to meet Dan.

She was early, so it gave her a chance to look around the outside buildings and the garden which was both front and back and quite large. An outbuilding which looked like it was falling down in the back garden could be replaced with a summer house which she had always wanted. The garage was brick built and still looked okay but Dan would check it out for her. The gardens were overgrown and had been neglected over the years but with some tender loving care she was sure it would look splendid. There was space between neighbours as well which she liked. Then she heard a engine, not a car, more like a van so she walked to the front of the property and Dan was just getting out of his van.

Sally walked up to him, "Nice to see you again Dan but where is the Estate Agent?"

Dan replied, "Not here, he actually let me have the key," jingling the keys in his jacket pocket. She laughed. He was a charmer. He gave her a hug and they talked about what she had been up to since he last saw her then turned his head towards the cottage.

"Nice, but a big project or do you have other plans?" he said, smiling, as he knew what she was like. He thought of her as a nomad, always moving from one place to another. She could not settle.

He took the keys and she followed him into the cottage. He was impressed by the sizes of the rooms and also the potential which she always envisaged with each project. The kitchen was dark but the potential of opening up the window into French doors could solve that problem. She had the eye from turning a hovel into a master piece which anybody would love to live in, her magic touch was endless.

They then went upstairs, creaking steps up the staircase as they ascended but they could be sorted. There were three good bedrooms and a large bathroom with separate toilet. She pulled him into the largest bedrooms and asked, "What do you think? Could we get an ensuite in here, or walk in wardrobe?"

He pulled a face. "For you or the future client?" he said. She gave him a playful push. They then came out onto the landing and he spotted the loft hatch. He went off to get his ladders, torch and tools. When he came back he went up the ladders and into the loft. She would have to wait, so she wandered around upstairs looking into the rooms.

She was in the bathroom with the tape measure out looking at moving things around and where all the pipes were and noted that the floor had floorboards which was good. Dan called out to her so she went onto the landing where he was folding up the ladders as he had finished then said, "Looks very sound up there, it could have been treated already so ask if the owners have a certificate for the work." He went on to say if they hadn't he would suggest she get it done for peace of mind. He gave her a figure but said to get a proper quote.

The next thing was him getting on the roof to check chimney and roof tiles. They walked outside to the van as he got the larger ladders out and turned to her and said, "If I was you I would take the ivy down and then the bricks will probably need pointing as well afterwards." He also gave her a pair of secateurs to cut the rambling rose in the back garden down, then he could check it had not damaged anything while he was around. He handed her them and he headed for the roof. She went round the back. He had a pair of gloves with the secateurs so she was alright.

She turned to go into the back garden to cut the rose down and nearly fell over the gentleman that was standing there in front of her. They both jumped back in surprise. He introduced himself as Ralph her next door neighbour. She thought to herself maybe a nosey one? She said, "How can I help you?"

He replied, "I wondered if you were buying the cottage, as it's haunted you know, by the previous owner. He was killed inside the cottage."

Sally laughed. "Well I will be company for the ghost then as I am buying the cottage."

He looked disappointed that he had not shocked her, and she turned, excusing herself, and went round the back of the cottage into the garden to deal with the rambling rose at the window. She got stuck into it and was in a world of her own when Dan made her jump.

"Sorry, I thought you would have heard me coming to see what you were up to," Dan said, looking at her handy work. It made a great difference and there was no stone damage from it. The roots had only lifted the patio a bit which she would probably make bigger anyway. Dan continued and said that the roof was fine except that the chimney needed pointing and a cover to stop birds nesting inside to be put in place. He also said the chimney would want sweeping as well.

She told Dan about her encounter with the next door neighbour and the ghost story he told her. He just laughed and said that he was finished and would give her a report of the work as soon as possible. He would email it to her then she could discuss it further with the Estate Agent. He then gave her a key to the cottage so she could return it for him, and they both left.

She arrived at the Estate Agent and told them she would pop in to see them tomorrow with the revised offer, taking into account the work that would be required to do according to the surveyor's report. The guy said that was fine and she left. She decided to go to other agents to see if they had cottages with similar need for work to make a comparison. It would also help her in case she wanted to sell it on after carrying out the work needed.

That was why she was good at what she did. She was thorough and her Dad would be proud of her achievements. She found another agent who was helpful to her needs and she made notes and took some details. She made some mental calculations on what would be the cost of what Dan had found. She then decided what reduction in her offer to cover her cost of works that need to be carried out. She went to her room and set about putting the figures into the computer, then she got the figure she would put forward to the agent tomorrow but would wait to see what Dan's report had before she went to the agents.

She was up bright and early the next day and was hoping things would go smoothly, but before she went to the Estate Agents she would do some more research on other cottages. She came across lovely cottages that she could see had been done up and it also gave her ideas of what to do with hers. Ideas like maybe a jack and jill bathroom or making an ensuite in the large bedroom, lots of ideas. She had Dan's email and knew what she wanted to offer on the cottage, and so shut the computer down and headed to the Estate Agent once she had had her breakfast.

Once she was finished she headed to the agents. Opening the door to the office she saw the guy she had previously spoken to and said good morning. He gestured for her to take a seat, which she did.

Sally then said, "I want to review my offer because of the amount of work which the surveyor has pointed out to me, and I also need details on the boiler as well. I need the age and whether it has been serviced, and whether there has been wood treatment carried out."

The guy, name of Clive, said he understood but could he have a copy of the report for the owners and gave her an email address to send it to, which Sally did for him and then stated what she was prepared to offer taking the work into consideration. He continued to talk with her, stating it would be a cash purchase on condition of a quick completion. He took all her details and said he would get back to her as soon as possible. He was not sure how long it would take and she would have to be patient. She thanked Clive and left the office and headed for the other agent. She thought it would be a good idea to view the cottage that had been done up, as she had nothing better to do.

On her way she passed the café she had used before, and decided she would go in for a coffee and do some work in her note book for the project. She went in and sat down and ended up ordering a scone to go with her coffee as they looked so good. She set to putting figures down of her budget which she tried to adhere to, but sometimes it would run away with her and she would end up making a loss, but only rarely. She planned what she was going to do as she had done on so many projects in the past.

She had a caravan which she would bring down to live in, while the work was being carried out. She was used to slumming it when she had a project on as long as the weather was not too cold and wet, then it would be uncomfortable and she would go into bed and breakfast places instead. She ate her scone and scribbled notes for herself and drank the coffee. Her phone rang. It was the Estate agent Clive who had a couple of questions for her. He wanted to know whether she was sole purchaser and needed her solicitor's details as well so Sally said, "So is the offer accepted then?"

Clive replied, "Well there had been no other interested parties and you are the only one, so we have advised our client to accept your offer, especially since the property had been on the market some time."

Sally gave him the details he wanted and said he would confirm everything with her once they confirmed acceptance of the offer. She finished the call and now needed to ring her solicitor but rang Jim the accountant first to confirm the monies for the cottage. He picked up the phone and Sally said, "Hi, Jim it's about the purchase of the cottage. What do you think? Put it in my name or the Company?"

He consulted the books and noticed she had not had a property in her name for a long time, and replied, "Well, are you going to live there?"

Silence for a moment. "Come on Sally take the plunge, give it a year at least. It is about time you settled down in a place," he said.

"You're right, Jim I should take the plunge, and it is idyllic. Okay, well in my name it will be. Can you contact Craig, the solicitor for me?" she said.

Jim said, "Not a problem. Just email the details across to me and I will forward it to Craig for you."

She thanked him and said she would be in touch. She finished on the phone, paid the bill and left the café. She was walking towards the other Estate agent when her phone rang again and it was Clive. The offer has been agreed, the boiler had only been installed two years ago but no certificates for the wood preservation. She told him that was fine with her and gave him all her personal details he had not got so far.

Great. Now things would move fast as it was a cash purchase, and she needed to organise the work force so that she could get things done as soon as possible. She headed to the Estate agent, to look at this cottage they were selling already done up for ideas.

Chapter 3

Time ticked slowly for Sally. She wanted to get her teeth into the project and she was impatient. She had agreed with the owners that once exchange of contracts had happened she could put her caravan on the long drive to the cottage, and also arrange for a skip as well so that she could start exploring the overgrown garden at the back.

She had her team, Benny and Franky, booked in to start stripping the place and had ordered the bathroom suites and kitchen. There would be a slight delay on some of the things but she could work round that. She had done this so many times now it was like second nature and having a reliable team working for her was important.

She was back at her base office when she took the call to say she had exchanged contracts and looked out the window of the office into the yard at her old faithful caravan that had been up and down the country over the last five years. In the next few months it would be her home. It felt different this time but was not sure why; a little apprehensive on committing to live in the cottage maybe?

She went down to the truck, loaded up with tools and hitched the caravan which had already been packed. She would take three hours to get there and could not wait. The journey was uneventful and when she arrived outside the cottage she felt a shiver, but was not sure why. She backed it up the drive and unhitched the truck. There was an outside tap for water and she would live simply until she could access the electricity from the house. She had food. What more could she want?

She set things up and was just sitting down to a mug of tea and toast when someone tapped on the door. "Typical," she said out loud and went to open the door. It was the neighbour again who she had encountered previously.

He said, "I warned you about this house but you took no heed. Woe be tide you." He turned and walked away. Sally thought, very strange. She thought he might have come to complain about the caravan, but this person that died in the cottage he was more bothered about warning her about. She shut the door and went back to her tea and toast, dismissing what he had said and planned what she was going to do tomorrow.

The back garden had been neglected and she would work some of her frustration off doing the work in there tomorrow with her tools she had brought down with her.

That evening and night nothing happened so she got up next morning, had her breakfast and went to start work on the garden. The weather was kind to her. It was cool but the sun came out occasionally. She started with layers of clothes and as she worked she took a layer off until she was down to her t shirt. She wore heavy duty gloves, especially when handling the rose, and made sure she did not scratch her arms.

A man's voice called her name as she was knee deep in a hole digging the roots of the rambling rose. The voice got nearer as it came round the back into the garden. Then when he saw her he gave out a wolf whistle. She looked up. She looked sweaty on her body with her hair tied back and dirt on her face.

The guy said, "You look as if you know what you are doing, but I have a skip for you I think."

She smiled, "Yes it is for me, thanks, you could give me a hand you know, it won't hurt you."

He laughed and turned to go back to the front with her following him. When she saw the skip it was just the right size. She thought, how can a woman get excited over a skip. She shook her head. She showed him where to drop it, and after he had, he came to her with the paperwork to sign. She took it and said, "You came recommended so here's hoping you can keep up with us in supplying many more as we work quickly once we get started on a property."

He replied, "Just give us twenty four hour-notice and we will be at your command."

He bowed and she laughed, "You are welcome to come to my house-warming when it's finished. I like you, good sense of humour."

She signed the paperwork and passed it back to him. "See you soon," he said and then left. Sally turned and went into the caravan to put the invoice she had signed into the file and then decided to make herself a drink. She sat down to drink the coffee, and pulled a piece of paper to her and started sketching her plan for the back garden which she had in her head. She would want certain plants if she was going to live here to make it her home. She was a white witch and needed certain herbs and plants to use. Not many people knew what she was but she used her skills when she could help people along the way.

She started writing at the top of the sketch plants she wanted; jasmine, lavender, periwinkle, sage, rosemary but also poppy, wolfbane, mandrake, but had to be careful with the poisonous ones. She also wanted blackthorn and rowan as rowan branches she would use to lay across the lintels on solstice days to reinforce the beneficial qualities of the plants and to bestow good fortune on the house. She would add these to the garden and might have to remove some to make space for the ones she wanted. She might discover a rowan but needed to clear the undergrowth before she could get close enough to it to make sure.

Then there was the dilapidated shed affair in the garden which she would remove and put a lovely summer house she could sit in when it's a bit chilly to sit outside and be sheltered. At this rate she might have to get in touch with Mark her landscaper she used to help with the heavy stuff she thought. He would be fine as long as she fed him, and he would always be available at weekends for her. She finished the sketch, rolled up the paper, put it away and decided to eat before she started working again.

She grabbed a quick sandwich and went back to tackle the rambling rose. By the time she had dug it out she had to move several patio slabs. Luckily for her they were the small ones and after she had removed the root and dragged it to the skip at the front she decided to clean herself up and go to the local pub for something to eat. After a lovely meal she came back and went to bed.

The next morning she woke feeling okay after having a good night's sleep ready for her to tackle the garden again. She had breakfast, a coffee and then took her plan out with her into the back garden. She cast her eye over the over grown garden which looked neglected and imagined her plan. She had a lot of work to do before she could order her plants and trees, but she had time on her side.

Chapter 4

The morning she received the phone call from the Solicitors to say the house was hers was very exciting, more so than usual. This house would be different she felt. The agent came out to the cottage and handed over all the keys and wished her luck with her project. This is when the hard work starts, she thought.

She rang Benny to let them know and he said they would both be down on Monday to start work. Dan her surveyor had organised drawings for her internal schemes from her sketches she had sent him, so she had ordered everything, so it was go from here for the cottage.

The garden was coming along but needed some hard landscaping work so she contacted Mark. She told him about this project and gave him an idea of what she was looking for and measurements of the areas that needed paving. He had worked with her before and knew what materials she liked. He said he would come down next weekend to make a start which she thanked him for. The trees and plants she had managed to get from the nursery but the more 'special' plants she had to get by mail order.

That evening she celebrated the purchase with a take away and a bottle of bubbly. Normally she would have a beer but this time as it was going to be her cottage. She thought bubbly was the order of the day.

Saturday morning she woke with the sun shining through the window of the caravan. She got up and dressed and went to explore the cottage, taking in every detail as she walked through the front. It seemed different this time, as she walked slowly round, walking into each room and visualising her plans.

She walked up the stairs and into one of the bedrooms when a cold shiver ran up her spine. The air became cold, enough to notice her breath in the air. She was not scared at all as she had to deal with ghosts/spirits whatever people want to call them. She walked towards the window and pulled the curtains open as sunlight shone across the room. The room was now back to the normal temperature. She thought to herself that maybe a spell to keep the ghostly presence away was needed. She would see.

She headed downstairs, shut the door and headed back to the garden, as the weather was looking good for today. She worked hard over the weekend, clearing the beds and removing shrubs that were not needed, and found the rowan tree which was just needing some branches cut and tidied. The lawn needed feeding, but after it had been cut several times it would soon look better. She would feed it in the autumn when all the work was finished and she had time to do the nice things in the garden.

The weekend was soon over and come Monday morning the troops arrived, Benny and Franky to be exact. It was good to see her team again and they said they would sleep in the house while they worked and she said that was fine by her. Before they started they had a meeting in the caravan to go over the project, taking one room at a time, the kitchen and bathrooms being the priority but as well as all the other rooms. They walked into the cottage and started in the lounge where the windows and radiators were okay, but she had second thoughts on the fireplace and said it had to go and she would go for a wood burning stove instead as it had an open chimney. She brought out her shopping list and added it to it.

Then the small room which was to be her study she turned to Benny, "Do you think, instead of the window, French doors as it would bring in more light?"

He nodded and took out the tape measure and made notes, looked up and smiled at her. "Okay we can get a double French door in so we will do that for you. We do have to make a profit you know, but we will adjust the price for you." They both laughed and she thanked him for his patience as usual.

They moved to the kitchen which seemed lighter since she removed the rambling rose away from the other end of the room. She was still after bifold doors to replace the French doors. They had agreed with her previously about them and then turned their attention to the design of the kitchen and then the boiler, which they agreed as it was only two years old it would be silly not to keep it. The wiring would be updated though.

They then went upstairs and into the bedrooms with curtains open, marking the power points to double in each room until they got to the small room with curtains closed, air cold and chilly, enough to notice your breath, but the guys did not notice it. So she pulled the curtains open, which changed the air again to normal. She would have to watch things, especially with the guys sleeping in the cottage. They continued into the bathroom, talking and measuring as they went. She asked about fitting in an ensuite into the largest bedroom and they said they would measure up and cost it out for her. She said she was sure that the price would be fine, it was a case of space to do it.

When they had finished the walk round she left the

guys to make a start. She needed to get some history on the house to see who the spirit was and how she was going to deal with it. She told them she was off to town and to ring her if they had any problems. She set off and headed for the Estate Agent to see if they could give her any details of the previous owners.

She arrived in town and headed for the agents and found Clive, who she asked about the history of the cottage, as she was interested in knowing who lived there in the past. He was very forthcoming, as it was gossip about what happened in the house. It seemed the owner's body was discovered by a neighbour some weeks after he died and the police were called in. The postmortem was inconclusive how he died due to the time lapsed. There were no marks on the body and the rumours were that a relative poisoned him. Sally thought, very interesting. Could it point to the ghost/spirit not able to move on due to it wanting revenge? She would speak to a friend who was also a white witch for help.

She rang her friend Fiona. No answer, so she left a message. It had been a few years since she had been in touch with her and that was when she had a similar situation. That was the problem, buying old properties with history. She would wait for her to get back to her and hoped it was not too long.

She headed back to the cottage after picking up a few groceries she needed. When she arrived there were vans and trucks parked outside the cottage and the drive, so she knew things were moving as always. They would soon be gone and that is why she loved working with Benny and Franky, as they were so organised, like her.

She parked her truck and went to explore what was happening. She was met at the door by Benny who advised her not to go in just yet as there were plumbers and electricians in the property plus they had just sprayed the roof trusses in the loft. She knew that but she would always try to get in. Seeing she wasn't wanted, she stepped back when Benny said something about the guy doing the damp proof course injection round the back of the house wanting to see her.

Sally asked, "Is there a problem?"

Benny replied, "Not sure but they wanted to speak to you as soon as you were back."

She thanked him and walked round to the back of the house where she heard raised voices, which went quiet when they saw her.

She said, "You wanted to see me, is there a problem you have found?"

One of the guys pointed to the ground and her eyes followed where he was pointing to. They had, in the process of digging down to see if a previous damp proof course had been covered up with earth, exposed what looked like something grey/white. She went over and bent down to have a closer look. Yes it did look like a bone, which would have spooked them a little, and she started to clear more soil away with her hand and then the trowel they handed her. She carefully exposed the bone which was about six to nine inches long and carefully lifted it.

The guys stepped back and said, "Do you think it's human?"

Sally replied, "No looks like an animal bone so you are okay you haven't dug up a part of a body," turning it in her fingers.

They looked relieved and she said they could go ahead and continue as it was not a body they had found. They laughed nervously. She told them they had been reading too many murder stories and then turned and left them too it.

She found Benny again and told him about the guys and what they had thought they had found, he laughed as well. He said she could have a quick guided tour with him, but not all the house at the moment, as too much was going on. She noticed no cold spots in the rooms they went in and Benny had not mentioned any strange things so maybe she was mistaken. She would see.

Chapter 5

Many weeks went by and the work progressed well. The garden was taking shape with a new patio and the old outbuildings removed. A new summer house was in its place, which Sally had painted. Things were taking shape both inside and outside the cottage.

Fiona had been in touch with her and they had a long talk about the possibility of a spirit in the house, and so she gave her a spell she could use to protect the home from physical and non-physical entities which she would use if necessary. Fiona also offered to come and help if it became a bigger problem. Sally hoped it was not a revengeful spirit, but she would wait to see how things developed.

All the plumbing, electrics and plastering was done, with the bathroom and ensuite finished upstairs and only the tiles in the kitchen needed finishing. The walls in the bedrooms had been painted as well. All that was needed was cleaning floors up there and carpets could go down. It was looking good, and it had worked well upstairs with an ensuite and walk in wardrobe which she had always wanted. Yes, she could picture herself living in this cottage for some time. Maybe after losing her father she had found her home again, to settle for some time to come.

Downstairs the kitchen/diner had worked well and her new fireplace in the lounge would be cosy in winter for her. Again the floors would need cleaning and then she could organise the carpets and flooring to go down. Benny broke into her thoughts as she sat in the garden sunning herself, calling her name.

She looked up to see Benny was standing next to her, "What is the matter?" she said, looking at him, as all the colour had drained from his face. "Are you all right. You look as if you have seen a ghost." She gave a half laugh when she realised what she had said.

Benny said, "This may sound weird but I think I saw a figure that looked transparent, upstairs in one of the bedrooms. It hung about for a few seconds but I definitely saw something."

She reassured Benny it could have been the way the light shone through the window, but he was not having any of it and wanted her to go upstairs to look. She left the garden with him and walked into the cottage together, and they both walked slowly up the stairs, waiting to come across cold spots as they walked. They looked in all the bedrooms and everything seemed normal temperature, no cold spots. He seemed reassured and came back down with her and continued the tiling in the kitchen. She decided that she would start cleaning the floors upstairs tomorrow herself, just in case anything more spooky happened.

The morning came and she started cleaning the floors and windows, just how she would want it doing. She broke off during the day, and went and sat downstairs with Benny and Franky to discuss things. It was while they were talking and having a coffee break they heard a noise upstairs. Sally dismissed it, saying her tools had probably fallen over. There was nothing more and when she went back to finish, sure enough two items propped up on the wall had fallen over. She thought nothing more and went to finish off the bathroom cleaning. While doing so the lovely mirror she had installed steamed up. As she turned round she found a message was written on the mirror in the steam she had created, 'Help me.' A shiver went down her spine and even with the warmth of the steam she felt cold. She hurried to open the window and soon the mirror was clear. She definitely had to speak to Fiona about this now, especially as she was going to live there. She did have the spell but thought that the spirit was trying to contact her and communicate something she needed to know. She was not sure.

The next two days passed with no incidents and she relaxed a little more. She organised for the flooring to go down upstairs while she finished cleaning the downstairs. Now everything was finished, Benny had stayed back so he could sort the doors once the flooring was down and he was in the caravan doing the final accounts when the neighbour knocked on the door and had a chat with him.

The neighbour said, "Very impressed on the work you have done and how quickly."

Benny replied, "Sally does this type of job all the time, it's her business and we have been working with her for some years now. This time she will be living in the cottage."

The neighbour looked surprise and said, "What about the rumours of the house being haunted?"

Benny laughed, "That would be silly believing that sort of thing wouldn't it?"

The neighbour just shrugged his shoulders and walked away. Benny thought for a few minutes was that what I really saw, no can't be and then got on with his paperwork.

Sally was in the lounge when she saw the neighbour head for the caravan, but he must have been happy with Benny as he was walking away again now, so did not want her. She was thinking to herself about trying the spell tonight while Benny was staying at the B&B down the road, probably after they had had a meal together first. That was the plan.

Sally cooked them a simple meal in the caravan and then Benny wished her good night and headed to the B&B, but probably calling at the pub for a pint as well. She looked around for the items she needed, white candles and the spell of course. She was good at meditation and visualising and was calm in herself. She walked into the cottage and into the lounge, setting things down on the floor and returning to lock the front door, as she did not want disturbing, and returned to set things up the way she needed.

She would light the candle first, sitting crossed legged next to it, focusing on the flame and chanting her words, and then visualising the wayward spirit floating upwards towards the light of the candle. Yes she was ready to do this. She lit her candle and settled herself on the cushion she had brought as the floor was too cold to sit directly on. She was ready to start.

She said, "Heaven's blessings do descend, Heaven's gates are open wide, spirit fly away, spirit go I say. Be gone now for evermore, be gone, be gone."

She repeated it three more times and as she did she felt a calm descend upon her. It felt like a warm liquid had washed over her. She closed her eyes and her breathing became slow and calm. She must have been like that for ten minutes, for when she opened her eyes the candle had burnt down more than usual. She blew the candle out, then wetting her fingers made sure it was totally out. She left the wax to cool and stood up, leaving it on the floor. Then she removed the cushion, and went into the hall to unlock the door. She opened it to leave, closing it behind her. She felt at peace with herself and hoped the spirit had gone. She went into the caravan and went to bed, wondering where her dreams would take her tonight.

The alarm woke her from her deep sleep and it took her sometime to wake herself up. A coffee would help she thought, and got herself one and took it back to bed. Once she had drunk half of it she was waking up, and would have to get herself dressed before Benny arrived that morning. They needed to thrash out the costings and agree on the final figures between them. This was the fun bit as she would always play the women card, but not too often. She might be able to get away with some things with him as she had worked with him for so long and before that he knew her father. She heard his van pull up.

He knocked and walked in. "Morning, and hopefully a good morning for us to sit down and work out the figures together," he said, smiling at her.

She said, "Okay you start while I make us both a coffee, black and strong, as I think we may need it," and laughed.

They had been pushing around the figures between them for an hour or so when a knock came at the door. She looked at her watch and then opened the door. It was the flooring guys, so Benny came out to talk to the guys while Sally opened the cottage and went into the lounge to remove the candle from the floor from last night. She put it on the kitchen window ledge out of the way and returned to the front door. Only to be met by Benny and the guys. She went over what goes where, and they both returned to the caravan while the guys started work in the cottage.

After another hour, both Benny and Sally had agreed with the costings with a little give on Benny's side this time. She said she would transfer the monies into the account shortly, once she had given Jim the final account. Benny left saying he would come back tomorrow to sort the doors for her. She thanked him and saw him off, and went to ring Jim who answered on the third ring.

She said, "Hi Jim, not busy are you?"

He laughed, "That's what you always think that you are the only one that is busy."

He asked, "What can I do for you."

She told him, "Well the project is nearly finished and I wanted you to pay Benny the last amount due to him as we have agreed the figures and everything is more or less finished. According to my calculations I am only £5,000 over my budget, so I am very pleased with myself."

He replied, "Well done you, better than the last two projects which you sold on. You are going to be living in this one, or so you said at the start of the project. Have you changed your mind?"

"No, like I said it was time for me to settle down and you are right I should make this one my home. It is what I was looking for a cottage," she answered. Jim thought maybe she is changing, he hoped so. She did find it hard after her Dad died to concentrate on projects but hopefully now she had turned a corner and would be putting down roots.

He agreed to do the money transfer for her in the next couple of days and then enquired when she would be moving from the other place where her stuff was. He needed to rent that out for her once she had moved out. She thought for a while.

Jim asked, "Are you still there?"

"Yes," she said, "Just thinking long and hard whether it would be better to sell it now."

Jim replied, "No you are okay with your cash flow at the moment so you could afford to rent it for say six months to a year before you sell it. So I would advise you to rent it."

She said, "Okay I will be guided by you as always. I will be out within the month. That will give me time to organise moving my stuff out." After she put the phone down she thought that would give her time to organise a house warming as well. She was deep in thought when a knock came at the door. The guys had finished upstairs and would be back next week to do downstairs, landing and stairs carpet as well as the wood flooring in the lounge.

She went into the cottage and went upstairs ready to get the cleaner out on the carpets when it hit her. She could see her breath in the cold air around her, the spell had not worked and the spirit had not moved on. She was so annoyed with herself she did not see the transparent figure in the room with her, but he was more solid now she thought. It was a little unnerving as she had not experienced this before. Usually they would move on with the spell. She had also heard that when spirits become more solid they can become more violent. She did not want that.

She moved slowly towards the doorway but the spirit stood in her way. What could she do without upsetting it any more? She needed to think fast. By the time she had time to think it was gone. At the same time someone was shouting her name from the hall. She did a double take, came to her senses, and called out she was coming, and as she descended the stairs came face to face with the neighbour.

He told her he was sorry to bother her but wanted to introduce himself to her as he had heard she was moving into the cottage. He was Alf and had lived in the area and the place next door all his life. She invited him to join her in the caravan for a cuppa, hoping she would get some information about the previous owners of the cottage.

They sat for a couple of hours and after he left she thought now she understood why the spirit could not move on. The story she had been half told was a tall tale. It seemed the couple who lived in the cottage were happily married for many years, until a few years ago when the wife walked out never to return and no body was found. The husband was broken hearted and after trying to find her gives up all hope and dies of a broken heart. Instead of his spirit moving on to a better place, his had remained. A body of his wife was found, but it was too late to tell the husband. Sally therefore had to convince the spirit (the husband) to let go to enable him to be re-united with his wife in the afterlife.

Now she knew what she must do and she would do it tonight to see if she could help the spirit move on. She had her book, candles and crystals. She was sure now it would work. She needed to do this if she was going to live in the cottage.

That evening she went into the cottage with all she needed and locked the door behind her. She lay the candles out and crystals, and lit the candles, then she started chanting the words.

She spoke softly, "Oh lonely spirit come to me so you can move on," chanting it a couple of times and then he appeared. She spoke calmly and softly. She hoped he understood her. Then she lit the special coloured candle and chanted, "Dear spirit hear my words. Your wife awaits you. Return to her arms. You must let go to join her forever, move towards the light and you will see her waiting for you in the light."

He moved towards the glowing light, the candle

was giving out which suddenly glowed even brighter and his spirit approached it. He seemed to know what he wanted to do, just join his wife again. His spirit entered the light and disappeared, leaving Sally with a feeling of contentment as she knew he had now moved on. She sat for a while with eyes closed then opened them. The glowing candle was now out and she blew the others out. Leaving them in place to cool and collecting her things, she thought she could now live in this place happily.

Chapter 6

Over the next few weeks everything progressed well. Sally moved her furniture in, which fitted well into the cottage and she only needed to buy a few pieces. She fitted the bedrooms out with new colour schemes and curtains and matching bedding. She was enjoying having a permanent home now. She loved the log burning stove in the lounge and the kitchen/diner with the bi-fold doors bringing her garden into her home. The garden was looking great and she enjoyed many days out there.

She had the house warming as she promised herself and invited all her work colleagues, neighbours and friends. They all got on, and she went to the kitchen to get herself another drink when Fiona came in to speak to her about the spirit.

Fiona said, "I presume things worked out with the spirit, seeing as you are happily moved into the cottage."

Sally said, "Yes, I had forgotten how it feels as a white witch to help spirits move on. I should not have stopped being involved with you and the group. It gave me peace I had not felt for a long time, in fact since Dad died."

Fiona gave her a hug and they both left the kitchen to join everyone in the other room.

Lightning Source UK Ltd.
Milton Keynes UK
UKOW01f1618150217
294501UK00001B/15/P